D1040878

The awkward morning-after...

At forty-three years old, Lilah had just made love to a man at dawn—in daylight—for the first time.

What was the morning-after etiquette? What should she say to him? Should she cook him breakfast? Light them both a cigarette? In movies, couples lay in bed smoking after lovemaking, but neither she nor Clint were smokers. Should she tell him she loved him?

Something told her that wasn't the thing to say to a man first thing in the morning.

Dear Reader,

How To Flirt. How To Boost Your Self-Esteem. How To Make Him Fall In Love With You. How To Lose Twenty Pounds In Twenty Minutes. Just a few headlines from fashion and beauty magazines—bibles for some women, waiting room fluff for others. I'm a devoted fan.

And so is Lilah McCord, a single mom who's had it with staying home alone on Saturday nights, in Cait London's supersexy novel *Every Girl's Guide To...* She studies articles on seduction, on being a "now-woman," on...*something* rough-and-rugged Clint Danner later uncovers in her apartment. Ever see a cowboy blush?

One way to ensure a blushproof romance is to date a man without meeting him. Laura Westin, lonely divorcée and title character of Toni Collins's terrific *Un*happily *Un*wed, falls in love via a computer singles network with a complete stranger—or so she thinks.

Next month, look for two Yours Truly titles by Dixie Browning and Kasey Michaels—two more entertaining and engaging romance novels about unexpectedly meeting, dating...and marrying Mr. Right.

Yours truly,

Melissa Senate

Editor

P.S. Please write me with your opinion of Yours Truly novels. I'd love to know what you think.

Please address questions and book requests to:
Silhouette Reader Service
U.S.: 3010 Walden Ave., P.O. Box 1325, Buffalo, NY 14269
Canadian: P.O. Box 609, Fort Erie, Ont. L2A 5X3

CAIT LONDON

Every Girl's Guide To...

Published by Silhouette Books
America's Publisher of Contemporary Romance

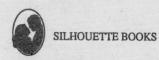 SILHOUETTE BOOKS

ISBN 0-373-52005-0

EVERY GIRL'S GUIDE TO...

Copyright © 1995 by Lois Kleinsasser

About the author

Why should men have all the fun in dating-game rules? When a woman reenters the dating lane, she's bound to discover changes of attitude. Oh-my-don'ts of yesterday can be shed. Today's woman is active, responsible, thorough and can go whole-hawg in every aspect of life (Note: I live in the Missouri Ozarks). All the challenged man needs to do is to keep up with her. And catch her. I hope you enjoy the fun and challenge as I did in *Every Girl's Guide To...*

Under another pseudonym, I write Western historical romances and enjoy bouncing "now-women's" attitudes back into the past century. How many women then could appreciatively pat their cowboy-sweetheart's backside and say, "Hey. I'm a partner in this relationship. Just maybe I'd like to romance you or change the pace. Do you prefer mountain biking or cooking Chinese or waltzing?"

I believe that today's women readers appreciate romances steeped in zippy, steamy humor and challenges. I appreciate my fans, reader-friends, who have provided me with awards and a lengthy bestselling list in Silhouette Desire and in Western historicals. Thank you, all.

Cait London has written eleven novels for Silhouette Desire. Look for her next book, *Miracles and Mistletoe*, from Silhouette Desire in December.

To Karla, who gave me the word *foofy*

1

"Well, June has been pretty dull so far. Reckon it's time to come out of the closet," Clint Danner said in the lazy, deep drawl that marked his deliberate, unshakable decisions. The nine-o'clock Saturday-morning "shooters" in Lilah's Billiards stopped playing eight ball to watch him with keen, narrow-eyed interest. Because when Clint used that dark-whiskey raspy tone and stood to his six-foot-three-inch height, he had conceived a plan and something was going to happen—"sure as shootin'." When Clint "set his mind to it," folks in Green Tomato, Oklahoma, waited for the earth to tremble and tornadoes to begin. He'd used that same lazy tone when he'd run a crooked land developer out of town and when he'd fought a cow-killer blizzard to save stranded cattle and when he'd rounded up Martin Lacy's rampaging bull.

Lilah stopped balancing her business's bank statement to watch Clint Danner. He methodically placed aside his cue stick in the personalized holder on the wall rack. Though his father and his brother had "passed on," their sticks remained on the rack, and Clint touched them briefly as he passed.

Lilah tapped the glass of mineral water sitting next to her and wondered just what closet Clint Danner wanted to exit. Clint's broad-shouldered, Westerner body wouldn't fit into a small space easily. At forty-six, he was lean and toughened by years of tending his tractor business and ranch in Oklahoma. The prairie's burning sun had etched lines around his eyes and hard times had carved grooves near his mouth. The overhead lighting glistened in the hair at Clint's temples and Lilah remembered how gray had suddenly appeared during the year he'd cared for his ailing wife.

Lilah had known Clint since she was three and he was six, and for the forty years that had intertwined their lives. She had married his best friend and he had married hers. Their children, Clint's two sons and her two daughters, had shared the same schools and childhood illnesses. Clint's wife, Betty, shared the same knoll in the cemetery as her husband, Jeff.

Clint's weather-darkened face wore an expression that caused Lilah to turn off her calculator and place her paperwork aside.

She recognized his steely, narrowed blue eyes, the lock of his jaw and the grim set of his mouth. Clint Danner had decided to make his move and the whole town would soon know what it was.

With the bearing of a man set on his course, Clint walked down the row of billiard tables, past the trophies Lilah's husband had won before the car accident had taken his life. Dressed in his usual plaid western shirt, worn jeans and expensive, polished boots, Clint moved in a lithe, long-legged stalk toward the bulletin board used to post messages.

The three elderly shooters who were Saturday-morning regulars crowded around Clint's broad shoulders. He scanned the board littered with wants and giveaways, shifted Ole's advertisement for a lawn mower to one side and tacked a sheet of paper to the corkboard.

Lilah found herself at his side, frowning at the big, bold, blocky print that marked Clint's life-style. She dipped under his arm and turned to look up at his expression; her face was level with his chest, which blocked the other men from her view. "You can't put that there."

Clint adjusted the paper with his hands, moving at the side of Lilah's head. He smoothed away a dark brown curl from the paper, glancing down her blouse and jean-clad body. He wrapped his fingers around her upper arm, easing her aside while he studied his handiwork. Lilah shivered; she'd just realized that Clint had used that same firm touch when he'd drawn her away from Jeff's grave. "Why can't I?" Clint was asking with interest as he studied the sign.

Lilah studied Clint's expression and recognized his determination. His lean, high cheekbones and slashing eyebrows resembled those of his ancestors; the Danner family bore the stubborn, blue eyes of the Welsh and the dark-skinned pride of the Cherokee who had survived the Trail of Tears. Their blood was forged in history and it was rumored that their backbones were dipped in steel. Anyone marrying into the Danner family had to have the spirit to meet the tempests.

She inhaled sharply; battling Clint was just what she intended to do now.

"*'Seeking single woman partner. Will teach to play. Clint Danner,'*" Lilah muttered. "Pool isn't the game you've been playing high and wide for years, Clint. You don't need to use my bulletin board to advertise for dates. It isn't proper. Angie won't like it."

Angie Wayne was out to marry Clint and everyone knew it. Including Lilah's married daughters, who worried about a man who was close to being a second father to them. Angie was there at Clint's free moments, twining her lush curves against his lean frame like a snake wrapping itself around its prey before it squashed the life—or life savings—from its victim. Rosemary, Lilah's daughter, had called Angie a "vampire who sucks men dry." Rosemary's husband had snickered then, the sound dying as she pinned him with a glare.

Lilah refused to think about exactly how Angie managed to age the men she lured into marriage and affairs. Though Clint hadn't seemed too badly drained after his dates with her.

But then, Clint was like the Oklahoma prairie—stoic, hard to read and persevering.

It was well-known in Green Tomato that a man could only persevere and survive so long under Angie's famed sizzling attention.

Jack Fain, a grizzled rancher, glanced warily up at Clint. "Women shouldn't play pool with men, Clint. It ain't natural. I've never played a woman in my life. They're emotional varmints, and built wrong to lean over a table. Has to do with top-heavy balance—" His leathery lips clamped shut as he glanced at Lilah's frown. "Pardon me, ma'am," he cooed sheepishly.

Lilah shook off the comment with a tight nod. Long ago, she'd gotten used to the male-dominated, pool-hall attitude.

"You smell good this morning, Lilah," Clint said pleasantly as he tilted his head to study his art work, then adjusted one corner higher.

"Soap," she returned flatly, unwilling to be distracted. She did note Clint's freshly showered scent and tightened her arms across her chest. "Clint, you should know better."

He glanced down her five-foot-six-inch body and his eyes sparkled with the taunt that she had ignored for years. "Is that Jamison guy still making eyes at you? I always wondered how a man could hitch up his pants that high and still be manly."

She angled her chin up at him and narrowed her eyes. She was not about to tell Clint anything about Edward Jamison, a nice man and one who she could not stand touching her. "None of your business. Do not try to avoid the subject, Clint. Remove your notice. It's all but saying—'' She threw out her hand, trying to think of a ladylike way to place her thoughts of Clint's availability.

"Yes?" he invited in an interested drawl, his gaze pinning the wedding band on her left hand. She couldn't bear to remove it, though it had been seven years since her husband's funeral. Clint had removed his band that same year, a year after his wife's death.

Old Sam, whose supposed age ranged from seventy to one hundred and ten, shook his head. "Women do not belong in pool halls—'' He met Lilah's frown and blinked owlishly. "Present company excepted, Lilah. Of course, you inherited the place by way of Jeff."

Lilah inhaled and looked up at Clint steadily. His dark scrutiny didn't unnerve her; she'd won her right to chastise him through the years. "Lilah's Billiards has never been a dating-game palace, Clint. You've dated everyone in the country. You just could be short of takers. Now wouldn't that be embarrassing?"

"We'll see. I'm culling them out and could have missed a few. This could draw them out of the woodwork," Clint drawled. He patted the page with his notice once, then glanced down at Lilah. "Take care of this want ad for me, will you? I've got to get to work."

Then Clint Danner sauntered out Lilah's Billiards' front door. She looked up at his advertisement and closed her eyes.

"She's counting," Old Sam noted in his rusty cowboy drawl.

"It's Clint. He does that to her sometimes," Jack stated sagely. "He's been culling the women for sure," he added, referring to discarding the imperfect of the selection. "Good old Angie is always there waiting for him to come back to her... That is, when she's available. She'll probably get him when he's too winded to run."

Determined to ignore the two old-timers, Lilah lifted her head and swished by them. "Culling," she muttered, slashing away at the figures on her notepad and suddenly realizing that she had placed the wrong numbers in the inventory list. "'Reckon it's time to come out of the closet.'"

Then the double front doors swung wide and Clint's western hat, broad shoulders and long legs appeared. June's early-morning sunlight framed his body as he walked straight to her, sweeping off his hat in a gentlemanly western manner as he moved past the snack counter. Lilah noted that Clint had moved through life in the same sweeping manner that made people stop and look. There was no way he could fit into any closet.

"Don't you take down my notice, Lilah McCord," he ordered, leveling a dark blue stare at her. "I mean business."

Lilah eased from the stool she had been using and met his stare. "Would I do that? I wouldn't want to interfere with your... playing pool."

"You should try it, Princess," he said tightly, then turned and left her staring at his very fit backside.

For the next hour, Lilah tried to concentrate on her ledgers as she did every Saturday morning, preparing for a busy weekend. Other than the video rental store, Lilah's Billiards offered the only entertainment in Green Tomato, and weekends made more profit than all the weekdays added together.

Unable to cope with the small ranch and memories after Jeff's death, she had moved into the upstairs apartment. Jeff had just begun his dream of a billiard parlor when the accident ended his life. Lilah had picked up his dream, cleaned the old tavern from top to bottom. She had fostered women's pool, thoroughly disgusting the old-timers of the town, and had changed the dingy beer-and-belch environment to one of light, quiet music, sodas and nonalcoholic beer. She had replaced the old-timers' beloved sexy female posters with aged photos of the homesteaders of Green Tomato. Plants occupied the brass spittoons and lace curtains strained the daylight filtering through the stained-glass windows. She had added a ''smoker's depot'' in another part of the parlor and a separate room filled with toys for children, which the Green Tomato's Tuesday Morning Ladies Shooters' League appreciated.

Clint's tractor business stood at the other end of the small, one-main-street town, a weathered stark gray board-and-brick building. It was much the same as the other stores lining the sunbaked street, but was surrounded by new and used farm equipment and a daily assortment of ranchers-come-to-town. His ranch had joined with Lilah and Jeff's, and now her daughter

Rosemary, and Rosemary's family, lived in the old McCord ranch house.

When Rosemary's baby, Lilah's first grandchild, was born during a blizzard, Clint had driven into Green Tomato for Lilah. He'd shoveled his truck out of snowbanks and managed to get her there in time to help with the difficult birth. The doctor was stranded at a distant ranch and Lilah, Clint and Rosemary's husband, Tad, had followed instructions and prayed that the telephone line would not break under the snow. Clint had held the newborn baby against him while Lilah worked with Rosemary, and later he had held Lilah on his lap while she cried herself asleep.

She'd helped with his sons' weddings and had seen his deep pride. She had seen him mourn his wife, Betty, and had seen him drunk and grimly determined not to cry.

Then she had seen the tears slide down his dark cheeks and his eyes close with stark agony.

Lilah had seen Clint enraged. It was a cold, determined rage, locking ice in his blue eyes when he'd learned that Olympia, her younger daughter, had been "attacked" on a date with a local boy. Olympia, home from her city job and college, had been shaken, but not hurt. Clint had "paid a friendly visit" to the twenty-year-old youth, who had thoroughly apologized and groveled and had since led an upstanding life in Green Tomato.

Clint was known to be a good neighbor who helped people when they needed it. A "man's man," he was a born-and-bred Westerner, sharing the unwritten code of men who held honor high.

Until it came to women.

Then tough Clint Danner had about as much sense as a— She refused to think of her longtime friend as the proverbial "bull in a cow pasture."

Lilah squeezed the carton of napkins in her fingers, strangling them. When it came to women, Clint had sampled the whole countryside in the past few years. After a year without Betty, he'd begun dating infrequently as everyone expected. But after his sons had moved away, Clint had given a new dimension to the term "widower."

His dates seemed to think he was very attractive, preening under his attention as he inevitably brought them to Lilah's.

"Culling," Lilah repeated darkly, realizing that while Clint's dates were parading bawdily through her mind, the parlor had begun to fill for Saturday-afternoon games.

A crowd of eyebrow-raising, giggling, teasing women had gathered around Clint's advertisement. Lilah poured freshly made sun tea into the dispenser and noted that "Big-Hair" Pilar Jones was salivating at the bulletin board. After two husbands and more lovers, Pilar knew men like she knew the prime stud bulls on her ranch land. She wiggled her tight jeans and penned in her name and telephone number on Clint's ad.

Lilah tapped her fingers and remembered when Pilar had attempted to lure Jeff away from marriage. At the time, Lilah had been grateful that Clint had shown a sudden interest in Pilar and had started dating her. There had been snickers across the countryside that Pilar was keeping him tired.

Then Clint had appeared at a local rodeo with a city woman from Tulsa—Ned Smith's widowed cousin. Pilar had acted pouty for a while and Clint had acted aloof...until he'd started dating a high-class, high-nose cousin of the Ameses.

"Ace." Lilah found herself muttering Clint's nickname in high school. When he'd made up his mind to succeed, he "aced" whatever his current goal was at the time.

Jeff had adored him and Clint had been his best man at their wedding.

Lilah respected Clint, his honor, his ties to the land and the community. She was grateful to him for helping in her time of loss, for helping with the ranch and for being there for her daughters.

They'd moved through life in the same town with an ease born of sharing both good and hard times.

But in the last four years, Clint had taken on an edge that raised her hackles.

She couldn't define his watchful, alert glances at her, nor did she particularly care for his nickname for her, "Princess." At forty-three, she was past her prime and watched from the sidelines as other women dated, married, divorced and remarried.

Lilah realized that she could not give another man the gentle companionable love she had given Jeff. She also knew that a relationship without her deepest commitment would be unfair.

Lilah filled the mustard container at the snack bar and began making sandwiches and hamburgers. She noticed Carl Wainwright sliding onto one of the stools in front of the bar. "Afternoon, Carl. How's it going?"

"Fine." A beefy, balding man, Carl ordered two hamburgers and double fries with a triple chocolate malt.

While Lilah was cooking, she saw a page slide from her facsimile machine. She let the burgers sizzle while she went to the small office area and read Clint's blocky letters.

Any takers yet? Save my usual pool table for me, will you? I'm tied up for a bit here. Be in around seven.

Clint.

Lilah inhaled and crumpled the page, tossing it into her trash, where Clint's advertisement might be if the women clustering and giggling around it weren't so thick.

"We haven't had a date for a while," Carl was saying when Lilah returned to the snack bar to serve his meal. "How about it, Lilah? I could bring a video up to your apartment and maybe some carry-out food for dinner."

"Thanks, but I'd better not." Their big "date" had consisted of his walking her home from the church social. Like everyone in Green Tomato, Carl was aware that she never invited men to her upstairs apartment. The last men in the apartment were her daughters' husbands and Clint, when they'd moved her furniture upstairs four years ago. She counted to ten when Pilar's husky, knowing laughter swirled through the parlor. Clint had been moving things around the countryside for years; shifting a few pieces of furniture was probably easier than peeling Pilar from him.

By four o'clock that afternoon, everyone in Green Tomato and the surrounding countryside knew that Clint Danner was looking for a new woman and if necessary, he would teach her how to play pool. Lilah had decided that it was time to have a chat with Mr. Culling-Them; she owed it to their families and the community in general.

Clint tightened the bolt on the tractor's repaired motor and straightened slowly. He narrowed his eyes against the sunset and looked at Lilah's place at the other end of the street. The old town looked rich in the dying golden sun, filled with memories of his parents bringing him and his brothers to town, of his old car—tied with empty cans and old shoes—whisking him away with his new bride, Betty. He saw a thirteen-year-old Lilah leaning close to the drugstore window and wishing for strawberry lipstick.

The parades filled with old cars, clowns and ghostly images of people dressed in their finest riding clothes rambled by him. The dry, hot wind rustled the old maple tree, reminding Clint of the years gone by. A quiet pain slid through him as he remembered the hearse driving Betty to her resting place—

Then he remembered Lilah this morning—her honey brown eyes, glinting with poorly shielded temper and ready to ignite. She'd looked the same when he was dating Angie; Lilah McCord had leveled a hot look at him and plopped a bottle of vitamins into his hand. "Better take care of yourself, Clint. You're aging fast," she'd said tightly.

He smiled briefly. Riling Lilah always improved his mood.

There was another look in Lilah's eyes that Clint longed for, that of a sleepy, well-satisfied woman who had spent the night in his arms.

She hadn't a clue that he'd been mooning over her for years, waiting for her to awaken to the present.

After Jeff died, Lilah had raised her daughters, then when they'd married, she had crawled up into the apartment above the pool hall and barricaded her heart. She'd fought the tavern crowd, who had wanted a free-wheeling beer-and-pool hangout, dug in her heels and worked for Jeff's dream, Lilah's Billiards. She'd dedicated herself to its success, and her life as a woman made for loving had ended. She delighted in her children and grandson, and held close to the ties that bound the town.

She clung to her safety, the apartment, barricading life from her like a princess locked in a tower.

Clint genuinely liked Lilah; he knew her strengths and her weaknesses, and her tender heart for those in need.

But her heart was wrapped tightly against living and loving and Clint had decided that now was the time to make his move. The idea had run through his mind for years, but he'd waited until Lilah had tucked away Jeff's memory.

Another ghostly hearse slid through the dusky sunlight, funeral flowers scenting the late-June day.

Jeff. Solid, gentle, loving Jeff McCord, who had doted on Lilah and his daughters. The day he was buried, Lilah had cried as though her heart were bleeding right into the grave with him and Clint had finally taken her arm, folding her close to him.

She'd felt like a little, broken bird, sobbing against his chest in the summer rain. She'd clutched his suit-jacket lapels and looked up at him with teary, wounded eyes. "Why?" she had asked raggedly. "Why did Jeff have to die in that car wreck. Why?"

Clint had lain beside her that night, after the doctor's medication had done its work. She had clung to him because he was a part of Jeff and because she couldn't bear to let go of her husband—

Just the year before, she'd held his hand as they'd placed Betty upon the cemetery knoll.

Lilah was like that—there when she needed to be, strong, kind...

Clint didn't want to take Jeff's place in Lilah's heart, nor did he want to share his relationship and bed with a memory. *Lilah needed stirring and Clint was up to the task.*

Clint intended to have Lilah and on his terms—love and marriage. He wanted to prove to her and himself that she hadn't thrown her heart into Jeff's grave. He wanted her to know that life and a future with one Clint Danner waited for her.... But first he had to stir her to life.

Through her life with Jeff, Lilah had retained her fresh, untouched allure, her almost virginal innocence. In her Sunday dress, usually a sprigged-and-ruffled cotton affair, Lilah didn't look like a grandmother—she looked like a woman born to make a man ache and take—

She'd blithely dropped every hint Clint had gently eased into her soft palm. She considered him to be her friend, her *brotherly* friend, while he had other intentions.

He'd decided that Lilah needed tempting like a heifer who has been left to roam the range overlong.

Just then, Angie's fast, red convertible purred to the curb near the reconditioned plows. She waved to him and Clint nodded. Angie Wayne was perfect fodder to stir Lilah, who called Angie "The Floozy." When he'd called, he'd made it very clear to Angie that he didn't want attachments, just a companionable date for an odd night, someone to play pool with at Lilah's, then to have a dance or two. Bored and between husbands and lovers, Angie had happily accepted as she had on previous occasions.

"Be right with you. I need to clean up a bit," Clint called.

"Huh. With Angie around, I wouldn't think you'd need to advertise," Lilah stated ominously as she stood by Clint and watched Angie bend over the pool table, lining up for a shot. Angie's daring cowgirl outfits always drew attention, from her tight-fitting jeans to her low-cut beaded-and-fringed blouses. Continuing on her way with the tray of nonalcoholic beer she was carrying, Lilah heard Mae Wheeler say, "They say that Angie had to lie on the bed to pull those tight jeans on."

When she returned with the empty tray, she glanced at Clint meaningfully. "One day, something is going to pop out of that blouse of hers and embarrass you silly."

"Uh-huh," Clint agreed in an absentminded tone as he studied Angie's lineup for her next shot. His gaze drifted down Angie's rounded backside and Lilah wondered if men knew which women wore panties with jeans and which ones didn't. Angie didn't, but she did wear a push-up bra, according to her beauty operator, Liz.

Lilah wondered moodily how many men had suffocated in the depths of Angie's endowments.

"How about a dance?" Clint was asking casually.

Lilah did not dance with her customers. Nor did she dance with anyone, anytime. The thought of a man's arms enclosing her, guiding her against his body, caused her to shiver.

After seven years, the feel of Jeff's nearness still moved strongly within her and she didn't want to replace the memory.

But Clint needed her help and he'd been Jeff's best friend. She owed taking care of him to Betty, her daughters and his sons. Now was as good a time as any to state her concerns to Clint. She could do that while they were dancing. "Meet you on the dance floor," she said, maneuvering through the heavy crowd of customers to deposit her tray and the new orders with Maxine. On busy nights, Maxine and Janey and sometimes Fred, Janey's husband, helped Lilah.

She glanced at Clint; his eyes locked with hers as he continued talking with Fred. His narrowed gaze followed her when she nodded and began walking onto the dance floor, weaving around the people swaying to the music. Lilah had a sense of a coming showdown, that her dance with Clint would have an impact on her life.

"Well?" he asked when she finally stood in front of him.

"Well, what?" she returned as a man's shoulder sent her against his body. Lilah's hands shot out to brace against Clint's hard chest. She jerked them away immediately and stepped back.

"You have to put your arms around me," Clint said slowly, watching her with guarded eyes. "Actually touch me."

"Oh...yes...of course. I know that," Lilah said and lifted her arms in the traditional shoulder-and-hand pose.

"Like this," Clint murmured, taking her hands and placing them behind his back. His arms enfolded her, his hands resting at her back.

Lilah hesitated, stiffened and watched the amusement slide into Clint's blue eyes. "You looked like that when you were ten and dangling a worm in front of me," she muttered, allowing her fingers to latch on to his tooled western belt.

"Mmm," Clint agreed lightly, sliding his hands to her back and drawing her closer until her breasts touched his chest. He tensed, his arms tightening around her, the muscles bulging for a heartbeat and reminding her of exactly how big and strong Clint was at close range. He began to negotiate her through a series of gentle, firmly guided waltz movements. The old-fashioned dance was elegant and easy in his arms, though Lilah had not danced since Jeff's death.

Lilah blinked at the view of his chest, the scents rising from his freshly showered body. "We've been friends for a long time, Clint. All of our lives. I'd like to talk with you," she said, looking up at him. "About your... physical... problem."

"What about it?" Clint had lowered his jaw to rest against her temple and his lips brushed her skin. He nuzzled her hair and inhaled slowly.

Lilah's senses darted into the past and back into the present; she remembered Clint holding Betty in this same, deliberate way, as if he treasured her above his life.

His hard thighs moved against her jean-clad ones and Lilah frowned slightly, aware of her softness and femininity against his body. No man, not even Jeff, had made her feel so fragile. She stiffened and moved slightly away. "Clint, do you know what is happening to you? Do you realize that you're going through some sort of midlife crisis and that you're exploring all these women—The Floozy—in an effort to prove something to yourself? Don't you realize what advertising for a woman partner can mean?"

"Tell me," he invited, his hands opening to span her waist and remaining on the upper curve of her hips.

"Don't be gooney," Lilah ordered, wiggling her hips in a hint that he should move his hands higher. Clint's fingers tightened momentarily, firmly, before he slid his hands to her back.

"You're going about this all wrong," she continued, when she saw him studying her face. His gaze touched her lips, which she licked in a sudden surge of awareness. Clint looked as though he wanted to kiss her, but then the way "...you've been acting, Clint, you'd want to kiss anything that wasn't a fence post. You're acting

primed and in heat," Lilah finished after realizing she
had been speaking her thoughts aloud.

"Is that so, Princess? Maybe you ought to try a little
heat," he murmured, leaning her over his arm, and
sliding his leg between her thighs.

"You know perfectly well that I'm not in the mar-
ket," she returned, forced to cling to him. "There isn't
anyone around who looks half-interesting."

She eased away from his body and forced herself not
to think about the thigh lodged firmly between hers. "I
act my age and you should, too. People will say
you're—" She tightened her lips. "I really don't want
to say what people say about your dating practices."

A dark flicker ran through Clint's blue eyes and his
jaw tightened. He pivoted her away from him and under his arm, then drew her back to him so strongly that
her body bumped his. He held her tightly against him.
She didn't understand the sudden anger humming
through him. "There are needs. People who live and
breathe have them every day, Lilah."

She flushed and straightened primly. "You don't have
to tell me that. One can only suppose what happens
when The Floozy is vamping you or you are—whatevering to her."

Clint's mouth softened and his gaze brushed her lips.
"Whatevering? Now that's an interesting term."

"Don't you tease me, Clint. My daughters are worried about you."

"Are you?" he asked gently, tugging her shoulder-
length curls.

"Of course I am. We've been friends for years," she answered immediately. "You were Jeff's friend and Betty was mine. We've been through a lot together."

"I'm not in need of a mother or a sister or a Dutch aunt," Clint stated grimly as Lilah felt his big hands caressing the length of her back.

"Clint Danner, you need help," Lilah stated darkly. No one could frustrate her as quickly as this man.

"Not likely," he retorted evenly. "I'm in the mood for romance. For earthshaking, sweat-making, body-heating, sweet, breathless kissing and heart-palpitating lovemaking followed by a week or so in a good strong bed. Of course, I'm hoping for a lot of promises of the heart along the way—the love-and-forever kind, the sweet nothings a man likes to hear on a cold night or in the light of day. I've got dreams of a woman coming to me, tossing away her past and wanting me in her future. There's more, but it's private. You'd blush if I told you."

Lilah stared up at him. "You are truly a sick man, Clint. One good dose of what you're talking about would cause you heart damage at your age. You were forty-six on your last birthday. I know because I frosted your cake." She ignored the length of his hard body bumping gently against hers. "Romance. You indulge in those activities and you'll not see another candle.... And I'm long past the blushing stage."

"Princess, the last time I checked, my body and heart rate were just fine," Clint murmured as he nibbled on her earlobe.

Lilah stopped moving.

Chills went down her spine and heat rose to her face. She trembled and quivered and gripped the anchor of Clint's belt with her fingertips. Though she knew she wasn't blushing, a sudden warmth moved slowly up her throat to her cheeks.

"...unclogs the arteries. You should try it," he whispered against her ear before his teeth caught her lobe again. "You know, Princess, I'd just really like to nibble a woman from her toes upward, kiss the back of her knees and—" Clint pressed the flat of his hand against her back, easing her breasts into his chest. He moved luxuriously as if fitting himself to her for a lifetime. "You are one soft lady, Lilah McCord."

Lilah blinked up at him and found him studying her. She also saw The Floozy glaring at her. Summoning her defenses and reminding herself of her mission to save her friend, Lilah frowned up at Clint. "Angie has already put two husbands in the grave. It is said that they expired in her... ah... heated clutches."

"If you're really worried about me, Princess, I'll try to avoid expiring," Clint agreed, and Lilah sensed that he had achieved an obscure victory. "But you might help me out of my lonely fits and need for breath-sucking, heart-racing romance."

"How?" she asked warily.

He studied the lights playing on her hair. "Oh, I don't know—I'll leave it up to you. Something to keep my mind busy so I won't dwell on that strong, creaking bed, kissing the backs of ladies' knees, and their other parts, losing myself in their soft purrs and cries of ecstasy."

"Oh, Clint. Is it that bad?" she asked, mortified that she had been so insensitive to whatever it was he was feeling at this time in his life. Clint was a widower and she could only guess at what a widower might feel in the lonely hours of the night; she had logged enough sleepless hours herself, but she had never come to the drastic needs that Clint had experienced. It had never occurred to her that he might need tending or cuddling. Lilah smoothed his back and allowed Clint to hold her close; she rested her head on his shoulder and realized she hadn't thought about his emptiness or needs— No wonder he was advertising, culling and dating the countryside, all in an effort to fill his loneliness.

A deep sense of shame overcame her; she had failed this man who had always been there for her and her family.

"I...I'm sorry, Clint. I had no idea," she whispered against his chest. The hard planes were familiar; she had dampened enough of his shirts in that first year alone. "I'll help you through this."

"Yes," he said firmly, holding her gently against him as a second record began in the jukebox. "Thank you."

A heartbeat later, Clint leaned down to whisper into her ear. "Why are you so quiet, Princess?"

"Thinking... I had no idea that you were so lonely. That you needed...ah...that your needs ran so strongly."

"Yes, I do admit they are very strong. They've been building for some time."

Lilah looked up at him warily. There were times when she trusted Clint absolutely, and times that his words seemed to hold a deeper meaning that slid by her. "At our ages, you should be past this...fever, Clint. Maybe you should see a doctor. It could be hormonal. They may have pills for that sort of thing now, you know. Maybe vitamins. Are you due for a checkup?"

"I don't think that is necessary," Clint murmured thoughtfully. "Are you shocked, Princess?" he asked with a teasing grin.

"I've seen you in a black rage, remember? Cursing a blue streak, snarling and ready to take the world apart with your fists when Betty— Who do you think threw that bucket of cold water on you the morning after your famous, rip-roaring toot? Everyone else was afraid to.... You've never been able to shock me, Clint."

"Oh, couldn't I?" he asked in a husky tone.

Lilah patted his back; she didn't understand his mood, the tense muscles rippling beneath her palm. "Never."

"Good enough," Clint said, then bent to kiss her lips lightly.

"The Floozy will make you pay for that," Lilah said breathlessly as she looked up into Clint's dark blue, burning gaze.

"Shoot," Clint whispered as though he were tossing his fate to the dry Oklahoma wind and kissed her again.

Then he drew away, ran a fingertip down her flushed cheek and winked. "Lilah McCord, you need kissing lessons."

2

At three o'clock the next morning, Lilah gave up trying to sleep and slid from her single bed. She'd chosen
the small bed to avoid having Jeff's empty space beside
her. She looked at his picture on her night table and
waited for the familiar pang of longing to squeeze her
heart.

Lilah stood in front of the full-length oval mirror, the
shadows of predawn wrapping around her pale body
sheathed in the style of nightgown that Jeff had always
preferred. The waltz-length rose-sprigged cotton gown
was plain and sweet; the mirror reflected a woman with
a heart-shaped face, tousled hair and huge, bewildered
eyes. She looked only a little older than Jeff's nine-
teen-year-old bride.

Her wedding ring caught the light as she moved her
fingertips across her lips. Clint had kissed her . . . twice.
She'd allowed him to hold her, to brush his hard lips
gently over hers.

"Just a kiss between friends," Lilah heard herself
whispering as the old maple tree brushed its leaves
against her window. "Surplus from Angie." Wrapping

her arms around herself, Lilah went to stand in front of the window that overlooked Green Tomato's main street.

Memories swirled around the street and she remembered her mother coming to town to choose a new length of cotton for Lilah's Sunday dress. The old blacksmith shop, once used by her father, was still busy during the weekdays. The grocery store had a new addition and the drugstore had added a big new neon sign; cherry limeades were still the soda counter's specialty.

She and Clint had grown up here. Their lives were like mountain streams, blending, separating, only to meet again and then flow separately into different courses. Her younger daughter was expecting a son now, and Clint's son, John, had just announced his wife's pregnancy. Lilah nestled comfortably in the past and sighed with the lonely weight of the future.

Clint wasn't comfortable with his widower status and was acting like a man half his age—at least dating like a younger man.

Lilah frowned at Clint's tractor business at the other end of the street, the one he had taken over from his father. "Culling," she muttered, thinking about Clint's necessary breathless palpitations and that strong bed. "He'll be lucky if he doesn't end up in the hospital to rest, living off vitamins to restore his strength. Of course, with the new staff of nurses, he would just proceed with his culling."

Lilah pushed back a heavy swathe of hair. The practical, multilayered, shoulder-length cut required little care and she had worn the style for years.

Years without Jeff.

They'd planned their lives, planned their retirement and travel. She'd never seen the gray enter his hair—

Theirs was a gentle, trusting love. Until one day at an intersection, a speeding dump truck filled with gravel for the Wilsons' new driveway ended everything.

Suddenly, Lilah felt very old and she slowly made her way back to the bed and slid between the rumpled sheets. She was still staring at the leaf patterns on the ceiling of her bedroom when the dawn rose slowly outside her window.

Sunday passed too slowly; the parlor was closed and yawned with emptiness as Lilah wandered through it. She cleaned the patio behind the building, repotted her jungle of plants and decided that she needed another lemon tree. She shampooed her hair and ironed her blouses and jeans. Finally, the hours stretched into evening and her daughters called with tales of their families.

Then the building was too quiet again and the night too long and empty. She sat in her rocking chair and overlooked the shadows of the town—two teenagers were kissing beneath the streetlight and an elderly couple was strolling arm in arm.

She found herself lifting the sand in a coffee table seashell and letting it slowly drift from her hand, like grains of time.

Monday evening at seven o'clock, Clint pushed open the parlor's double doors and walked through them, straight for her. He plopped his hat on the snack-bar counter and glared at her. "I couldn't do any work today. Every single woman in the countryside dropped by and some that weren't single," he stated flatly. "There are enough pies and cakes in my office to make it look like a bakery. Ed Jones's tractor overhaul had to wait."

"Oh, don't tell me Clint Danner has too many women running after him. And don't come to me with your problems. You know what I thought about your ad in the first place." Lilah patted his tanned hand. "Why don't you play a game? You'll feel better."

Clint's big, callused fingers trapped hers instantly. Surprised, she noted his dark expression—as if his problems were caused by her. "You're grouchy, Clint. Don't take it out on me."

"Why not, Princess?" he asked bluntly, his thumb caressing the skin of her inner wrist in a slow, hypnotic movement.

"Because *I* am not *your* problem. You have created your own mess by deciding to step out of whatever closet you thought you were in," she returned righteously and began tugging her hand free. Clint held it easily. "You're just as ornery as you ever were," Lilah stated. "Let go and stop calling me Princess."

"Are you going to dance with me later or not?" he asked flatly.

"After you play pool with all the names written on that cute little advertisement? No, I won't.... Don't you pick on my poor defenseless customers. And I won't put up with your grouchy moods, either. Take down your ad. It's a disgrace for a man your age to be acting like a lovesick boy."

"I've decided to get married," Clint said slowly, watching her intently. "Or get into a lifetime relationship just as good. What people call a 'significant other' arrangement might be just as good nowadays. I'd treat it just the same as marriage vows."

Lilah knew her fingers were trembling within his; she knew she was holding his hand, the security of Jeff's longtime friend...of her friend. "Oh?" she asked after clearing her tight throat.

She didn't want to lose him. "I'm glad," she murmured. "Anyone I know?"

"Could be. You'll know when I get the women culled out," Clint said easily and his eyes tasted her lips. His gaze moved down to the first button on her blouse and he touched it lightly. "Most women open a few of these. It's...inviting."

Lilah jerked her hand away. She clutched her trembling fingers tightly. "We're talking about your midlife behavior, Clint. Not my buttons."

"Okay, Princess," he drawled and humor lit his eyes.

Lilah resented his teasing. "We're both past the age of flirtation, Clint. At least I know I am—you seem to have a problem."

"I want a wife, a woman in my bed, Lilah," Clint stated, meeting her eyes until she looked away. "And I want a whole lot more than that, too. We didn't die with them," he said almost impatiently.

She shivered; lately, Clint had been unnerving her and when she was tired— His finger brushed the area beneath her eyes. "Sleeping okay?" he asked.

"Fine. I'm sleeping just fine," Lilah retorted. "You'd better get out your romantic-game calendar, Clint. Here comes Angie."

By Friday night, everyone in Green Tomato knew that Angie's claws weren't permanently lodged in Clint. "Big Hair" Pilar circled him once or twice and strutted off with a disgusted expression when he didn't pay attention to her. He'd played the availables and somehow managed to look so ornery that Lilah had allowed him to bully her into playing a game and later, dancing with him.

"You are not a happy man, Clint. You've been snapping at everyone, even Old Sam," Lilah said on Saturday night when she noticed the circles under his eyes. His expression was that of a man stretched to his limits. "If you don't mind eating late, come to dinner in an hour. We'll talk."

She had the distinct impression that Clint was suddenly alert, like a hunter picking up a scent. Though he hadn't moved, she was aware of the tense set of his body. "Would that mean your apartment, Princess?" he asked slowly.

She shrugged. "Someone has to take care of you. It might as well be me, until you get whatever is troubling you settled. I'll get Janey and Fred to close."

"Gee, thanks," he said. "I feel a heap better knowing that I'm your charity case."

"Well, maybe you just need a decent meal and a talk with someone who won't back off when you get surly. Beefsteak and fried potatoes without green vegetables isn't a good diet—don't expect it from me."

He smiled and something shifted warily within her. "I like dessert," he stated firmly as his hand wrapped around hers. "You realize what gossip this could stir up—me at your place, after hours?"

"No one will think a thing about it," Lilah said righteously and patted his hand. "We've been friends for years. Everyone knows that. It's not like we're... keeping company, or anything."

"Keeping company? People might say we're lovers," Clint murmured slowly, watching her. "That we're romantically involved."

He lifted an eyebrow. "They might even say we kiss and steam up the windows."

Lilah shook her head firmly. "No. No one would say that. They know how I feel about Jeff."

"Uh-huh. I know I sure do," Clint said tightly. "I've never known you to be a woman frightened of making changes."

Lilah folded her arms. "Clint. Some things don't change."

His jaw tightened and his eyes narrowed down at her. He glanced at the lines of men and women doing a fancy step beside one another. "I'll bet you can't line dance," he challenged, referring to the dance where men and women stood side by side and moved through intricate steps.

"Haven't needed to," she replied, not trusting his sudden grin. "I'm not on the line of cullables."

"There's culls and then there's culls," he stated obscurely. His fingers laced through hers and he tugged her slightly against him. She moved back a step and Clint smiled grimly. She didn't trust the way his smoky blue gaze locked with hers, as if he was set to have his way.

Clint removed his hat and stepped into Lilah's apartment. "I'm in here," Lilah called from the kitchen as he took in the spacious homey apartment, the sewing machine draped with cloth in the shadows. The scent of Lilah swirled around him, feminine and enticing.

Behind the couch stood a table cluttered with family photographs and he recognized himself, Betty, Jeff and Lilah at the county fair. There was Jeff holding a newborn daughter, and Lilah and Betty as teenagers mugging for the camera. Clint inhaled slowly, placing his hat near the photographs; he glanced at the seashells arranged on the coffee table, the sand and the starfish in the abalone shell. Then he entered the small, gleaming kitchen.

Lilah grinned at him. "Spaghetti. I canned the sauce last summer. The Jorgensons had too many tomatoes and gave me a whole bushel. It's not like the old days when I canned and sewed my life away. Now I like to can my favorites or to make jam for the kids. Dinner is ready."

He wanted to kiss her—to take her in his arms and hold her so tightly that the memories of Jeff's loving would blur. He wanted her to realize—

Lilah frowned slightly and placed her hand along his cheek. "Don't be uncomfortable, Clint. It's not like we're having a romantic rendezvous, or anything."

Nothing could have kept Clint from taking her wrist and drawing her palm to his lips. "I appreciate this."

"It's nothing. Just a friendly dinner and a video...." Lilah drew away quickly, hustling through setting the table and preparing the salad. During dinner, they talked quietly of the weather, of their children, and Clint thankfully noted that Lilah avoided the subject of his wife and her husband. Despite her protests, he helped her with the dishes, enjoying angling his body around hers in the small kitchen.

"I like seashells," she told him suddenly as they watched Humphrey Bogart pulling the *African Queen* down a leech-infested swamp.

As she explained how the dawn brought out the delicate pink lights in the conch shell, Clint smoothed her hair just once and very lightly. Lilah glanced at him, her smile gentle. ''Feeling better?''

Clint knew what would make him feel much better— to have Lilah look at him with the awareness that she just might be in the running for his ''significant other'' vacancy.

An hour later, he lay, dozing on the couch, wrapped in the scents and softness of Lilah nearby. She soothed him, he decided, when she wasn't exciting him. He'd logged hours of lost sleep over Lilah; he deserved a little soothing. He suddenly noticed that she was tugging off his boots and socks. She patted his head when he began to sit up. ''That's all right, Clint. You sleep on the couch tonight.''

Clint allowed himself a satisfied, drowsy smile when the door closed to her bedroom. If he wanted to, he could take himself home easily. But spending the night under the same roof as Lilah McCord was too enticing to miss. ''I've made it past the moat and into the tower,'' he whispered sleepily to the arrangement of shells.

''I knew it,'' Clint was saying in his deep, raspy tone as Lilah surfaced slowly from sleep. She smelled coffee and the distantly familiar scent of a freshly showered male.

Clint, dressed in his morning black stubble, bare chest and jeans, lounged at the end of her bed. Angular, bold and dark, his looks were dramatically male against her flowered-and-ruffled bedroom.

Lilah stared at his broad, deeply tanned chest lightly covered with hair and followed the view down to his flat stomach and the long length of jeans to his big, bare feet. He wiggled his toes as he sipped his coffee. While she floundered in sleep and noticed that there wasn't much room left in her bedroom with Clint in it, he drawled, "You're cute in the morning, Princess. All sweet and cuddly."

Lilah blinked and slowly drew the flower-spattered sheet up to her neck, concealing her modest nightgown. She peered at him uncertainly. She hadn't realized a man's beard could grow overnight to cover his jaw. Jeff had been blond— "Clint?"

His eyebrows went up. "Mmm?"

The tone of a sensually interested male wasn't so far in the past that she didn't recognize it. His eyes lingered on her mouth, then on her breasts, each one in turn, then slid slowly down her body. "Mmm," he murmured again, in the same luxurious, approving male tone.

Her body responded, surprising her as her breasts ached and hardened. Her nipples etched a pattern on the soft sheets.

Lilah considered her body's reactions and found them shocking.

Just for an instant, she'd wanted to rip away her gown and press her bare breasts against Clint's tanned-and-hairy chest.

She swallowed and found she had just trembled.

Lilah swallowed again and blinked, as a wave of guilt splashed over her— Clint needed her care, and his excess hormonal needs must have seeped momentarily to her.

A lady did not even think about boldly showing her needs—or loving in daylight.

She watched Clint slowly place his coffee cup next to hers on the bedside stand.

Then, Clint's light, teasing kiss flattened her to the bed. Her fingers gripped the sheets, just as she wanted to grasp his bare, gleaming shoulders.

The kiss changed, moved hot and stormy through her senses, dark and demanding, his mouth fitted to hers. Lilah held rigidly still, awash in uncertainty and stirring emotions. She tightened her hands into fists, crushing the sheet between them. Her eyes open, she watched Clint's black eyebrows draw together, his lashes lush and straight, framing dark, stormy blue eyes as he returned her stare.

Kissing Clint with her eyes open, his stare meeting hers brought a word to mind—erotic.

"Erotic" didn't fit in her life. She doubted that it fitted into Green Tomato, Oklahoma.

Neither did Clint's lips pushing at hers, seeking...

Lilah gasped for air when Clint eased a few inches away, bending over her. He tugged her hair gently. "You forget to breathe when you kiss. You turned red. Want to try again?"

"I...ah...no, thank you," she returned breathlessly, unable to force her eyes away from his.

At that moment, that fraction of a heartbeat, she wanted Clint's tall hard body lying over hers, heating the emptiness. She wanted him resting on her, squeezing out the loneliness— "Tell me what you want, Princess," Clint ordered huskily and she realized that his open hand lay on her stomach, warming, caressing her softness.

A memory zipped through her; Clint had lifted her bodily from the bed where she had lain for days after Jeff's funeral. He'd carried her, sheets, blankets and all to the ranch house's front porch and sat in the old rocker with her. He had rocked her for an hour while she watched her daughters skip rope, while the cattle left for the back pasture and the piglets scampered around the old sow. "Listen to the grass grow," he'd said over the *creak-creak* of the rocker. "Life is all around us, Lilah. Look at your girls. Look what you have. You're a strong woman. Jeff wouldn't want this..."

After another hour, Lilah had gathered her blankets and her dignity and had eased from his lap. "You've embarrassed me enough, Clint. I'm sure you have other things to do than rock a full-grown woman on the front porch. Why don't you go home now? I've got work to do."

"Good enough. I'll leave it up to you then," he'd said in a satisfied tone and had placed his hat on his head. He'd dipped the broad brim in the standard western greeting and without a second glance, had driven his pickup away from the McCord ranch.

Now the man sitting on her narrow bed, his hand splayed open on her stomach, was the same dear friend—gentle in his way, aggravating, respected and steadfast. The bonds of time entwined their lives, but a quivering awareness, silvery and thin, also slid between them, the glimmering, obscure facets frightening her. She placed her hand over his.

"I loved him so much," she whispered, the tears shimmering inside her, closing her throat. "I thought we would last forever."

Clint looked at the open window, the morning breeze moving the white lace curtains. He was silent for a minute, then he looked down at her, the angles of his face hard in the shadows. "You weren't buried with him, Lilah."

"Maybe not. But a part of me stopped living."

"Did it?" Clint demanded. Then he slowly shifted his length over her body, just the way she had shockingly wanted him to do moments ago.

The heavy secure strength she'd wanted pressing down on her was Clint. He'd cared for her in the difficult times and was her friend.

His hard chest pushed gently against her breasts, his hard thighs weighing hers. "Let's try this again," he said in an uneven tone as he framed her face with his hands and lowered his lips to hers. "Keep your eyes open, Lilah McCord, because I want you to know who you're kissing."

Then with the layers of cloth separating them, Clint gently arranged his legs between hers.

He slanted his lips against hers, paused, then slanted the other way. "Noses," he explained huskily. "Yours is short and cute, but mine isn't."

"Clint—" The hair on his chest rubbed the backs of her hands as she gripped the sheet.

"That's right. Clint. That's who is kissing you," he murmured softly, kissing the corners of her mouth and the tip of her nose. Then he kissed her again in a gentle seeking way that caused her to hold her breath—until she realized the movement caused her breasts to push up against him.

She lay rigidly beneath him and his face rested in the curve of her throat and shoulder. He moved luxuriously upon her, pressing deeper between her legs and Lilah blinked several times up at the ceiling as she recognized his body's desire and strength. She lifted a hand to move away from him and her fingers clung to his shoulder— Cords and muscles moved beneath her palm as it drifted to his back and Clint inhaled deeply. "Put your arms around me, Lilah," he whispered tautly against her throat.

"Loving isn't for daytime or Sunday mornings," she returned unsteadily and felt him smile slowly.

"Huh. What do you know about that," he murmured without question, as if the rule were new to him.

"You can't just mash me to the mattress, Clint. If you don't move, I may have to do something drastic," she threatened, aware that she couldn't shift Clint's strength and weight easily.

She also knew that part of her wanted him exactly where he was.

His finger strolled around the ruffled neckline of her simple nightgown. "This is sweet," he said with interest, then lay his head slowly, exactly, on her breasts and lightly nuzzled her as though making himself comfortable for eternity.

"Lord, Clint," she exclaimed tightly, afraid to breathe, as he rested on her. "Maybe you'd better go."

"Tell me to and I will," he said softly against the sheet over her breast.

Then he fitted his mouth over her softness and nibbled gently.

Lilah shivered and inhaled and her body tensed and quivered.

The bed seemed to rock beneath her.

When Clint gently bit her other breast, she heard herself releasing a long, high-pitched sigh.

He raised above her, his arms taut and corded with muscle beside her, his expression hard. "I don't need your sympathy, Lilah McCord," he stated bluntly as she dealt with the riveting sensations rocketing through her body.

"This is how I want it," he whispered rawly before framing her hot cheeks with his large, roughly callused palms. He kissed her in a way that wasn't brotherly or like a Dutch uncle.

In the next heartbeat, Clint was gone.

Lilah decided she had been dreaming—until she touched her swollen lips with her fingertips and looked at the two cups of coffee on the bedside table.

Jeff was smiling at her and she turned his framed photograph facedown on the lace doily. "Clint Danner is further gone than I thought," she muttered to the fluttering curtains at the open window. "He does need help. Apparently, The Floozy didn't drain all the juice out of him because he seems to have plenty of excess."

"Mother?" Olympia's worried voice slid over the telephone line. Lilah's younger daughter had probably been briefed by Rosemary, who had already called to see why her mother had missed church. She had been too shaken by her emotions to dress. "Rosemary said that Clint's pickup was in your parking lot all night. Is he okay? When was the last time you saw him? You don't think that he's rusting away at that ranch of his, do you?"

"He's not rusting," Lilah said slowly.

"I don't want anything to happen to Clint," Olympia said firmly. "Mom, you need to take better care of him after all he's done for us. Rosemary said he's dating that Angie person again. You know what a man-eater like that could do to a sweet person like Clint."

"It's a midlife thing, Olympia. Clint will be okay," Lilah murmured and wondered if *she* would. Her breasts felt heavy and sensitive. Her entire body seemed too tense.

She decided to wash and iron all of her curtains and double sugar-starch her ruffled doilies.

Clint rode his gelding to the back field and slipped from the saddle. He placed a boot on a fallen log and scanned the oil rigs moving silently like huge chickens pecking at the earth.

Lilah.

He'd pushed her this morning and he'd keep pushing her—until he'd torn away the shroud she clung to.

Reining in his need of her, to hold her, to touch her and tell her what was in his heart hadn't been easy. She'd lain all soft, big-eyed and stunned beneath him.

Clint closed his eyes, inhaling the evening air and remembering her scent.

That all-woman scent of Lilah McCord.

His eyes narrowed on the rolling prairie, this land that had meshed his life with Lilah's, the soil that had taken and had given.

His gaze swung toward Green Tomato. Lilah would be thinking now, sorting through what had happened this morning—he hoped she would be feeling . . .

She'd be tough to handle if she knew he wanted her.

A strong woman, Lilah would react to what had passed between them. He remembered her surprise and in the evening air, the high, tight keening sound at the back of her throat echoed in his mind.

Her lips hadn't pushed at his, hadn't opened and he'd made certain not to frighten her by tasting her with his tongue or by moving his weight too heavily against her.

She'd lain beneath him, tense, uncertain, and she hadn't moved away.

Clint smiled grimly. She didn't have the slightest notion of how to kiss or how to hold him.

He corrected the thought—how to hold him tight and open her mouth and give him what he'd needed for years.

But the trembling and the heat were there, layered by years and inhibitions. He intended to strip away what lay between them. It was time....

"Lilah McCord, I fear we are in for a fight," he said softly to the rising, huge silver moon. "Because you'll have to call it. You'll have to make your choice."

3

Missy Solomon leaned over the pool table and Clint's tall, rangy body framed hers as he showed her how to sight down her cue stick.

The Friday-evening crowd stared openly as Missy's wide blue eyes worshiped Clint's skills. The all-American, blond, Miss Apple Pie inhaled and clung to every word he drawled, and laughed up at him while they danced. Clearly, Clint had placed those stars in her eyes and the laughter on her glossy, innocent lips.

Despite her lack of sleep and tense nerves, Lilah noted that sweet, young Missy knew how to line dance expertly. Her jean-sheathed legs moved in perfect rhythm with Clint's long ones.

Lilah also knew that Missy was too sweet and young and untried for Clint's orneriness.

Saturday morning, Olympia and Rosemary called and told their mother that Clint and Missy's liaison would be a "disaster." Olympia said Missy was "foofy"—decorative and without an excess of brains. Rosemary demanded that her mother take action. She'd heard of older men losing their heads over younger women with small brains and lush curves. Rosemary, an expert on childbearing after one child, declared that Missy wanted a huge family—ten or so children—and that she would wear "poor old Clint" down to a "nubbin," then take his money and move on to a younger man. Rosemary was certain that Clint would not manage to break away from Missy's helpless tentacles and ordered her mother to protect Clint.

"How should I know what to do?" Rosemary had demanded in an exasperated tone. "Marie at the dry-goods store said that Missy bought a thong bikini and wants Clint to take her swimming.... Keep him busy, Mom. Missy thinks slow. She won't know anything is going on. Mom, do something. You owe it to poor old Clint."

"Poor old Clint," Lilah repeated Saturday night when Missy and Clint were playing pool and Missy snuggled close to him, asking him to show her how to make a difficult shot. Determined to protect her friend and his young disaster, Lilah edged between them with a tray of drinks and smiled tightly up at him.

He raised his eyebrows and with his hat tipped back, he looked rakishly young and daring—perfect for Missy.

He wasn't showing the effects of sleepless nights after his mashing of Lilah, while a tornado of emotions had run through her every minute and back again in the next heartbeat. Every beat of her heart told her that she was hovering at the edge of some frightening precipice and it all had to do with Clint's actions in her bed last

Sunday morning. He'd stunned her and she believed he'd acted out of loneliness. He'd stepped over the line of their friendship and yet he was the same old Clint.... *Poor* old Clint, she corrected mentally.

A tiny sting of anger zipped through Lilah. "Here, take this," she said to him, handing the tray to him. She flicked an impatient glance at Missy, whose blue eyes had widened. "Clint isn't a genius, Missy. Anyone can make that shot. Two ball into the side pocket."

Then Lilah proceeded to methodically clear the pool table of all balls, shooting them neatly into the pockets and calling the shots. She nodded and took the tray from Clint who was grinning widely. "There."

A half hour later, Lilah glared up at Clint who had placed his hands on either side of her head, trapping her in the narrow hallway leading to the storage room. She supposed he needed the wall's support after angling his body around Missy's. "You're taking me riding tomorrow afternoon, Clint," she stated, flattening her body—which had started humming with a strange electricity—away from his. She sensed that if his chest touched her breasts and his thighs touched hers, she'd zap him with a sheer jolt of...whatever. Her emotions were probably due to her anger with him. "I want to talk with you. I'll bring a picnic lunch."

He nodded, his dark blue eyes glinting with something she didn't understand. "Good enough."

"This is not a threesome, Clint. Missy is not invited."

"She'll be lonesome, Princess," he returned slowly, looking at her lips.

She wanted to grab him by the ears and pull his mouth down to hers and try some sucking herself— Lilah shook her head, clearing her thoughts. She had to save Clint and poor little Missy.

Clint bent to kiss her lightly—a friendly kiss, she decided. She was stunned as her lips pushed timidly at his of their own will, then he returned to astounding Missy with his expertise, wit and super-genius intelligence.

While Missy's high pitched giggles scraped her nerves, Lilah sensed that Clint was very pleased with himself. She looked at Missy's flowered western blouse and noted the top buttons were unfastened. Because it seemed rather close and warm in the billiard parlor that night, Lilah stealthily unbuttoned her first two buttons and found Clint staring at her from across the length of the room.

He looked her down, then up and time stood still as lightning seemed to crack through the distance between them. Lilah glared back at him; he was miffed by her interference. But when you're saving persons from certain disaster, you can't always let them run amok in midlife fantasies, she decided. Then Lilah tossed her head and turned away.

Late that night, Lilah stared up at her bedroom ceiling and wondered if Clint kissed Missy in the same sweet brush-brush of his hard mouth as he had kissed her. It seemed as though the suffering old polecat was so lonesome, he just had to kiss someone. She flopped onto her stomach and flopped back again, realized that she was hot and uncomfortable in her gown twisted around her legs and stripped it away.

She turned on her bedside lamp and lugged piles of women's magazines into her bed and curled beneath the sheet, skimming the "how-to" and "every girl's guide" articles and ads. She spotted a model with Missy's sweet innocence dressed in a bridal veil and little else; Lilah tossed that magazine to the floor. She opened another magazine and considered the exercises to keep her body sensually toned and tried a few of them, concentrating on the tightening and relaxing of intimate muscles. There was nothing difficult about tightening her buttocks and lifting them slowly off the bed. But she couldn't see herself biting Clint's lips to excite him. Or placing perfume on the insides of her elbows and between her breasts. Or taking a bath with three drops of erotic, male-alerting ylang-ylang oil and a room filled with candles.

The lingerie ads were standard, but an article on birth control stopped her.

She knew what those packets in the accompanying illustration contained though she hadn't seen the actual device. The packets seemed very flat and tiny.

The article recommended abstinence, but itemized the variety of colors and textures available in protection.

Lilah lay awake a long time after her eyes told her to rest. Her body hummed with an electricity that always brought her back to Clint.

She repeated the tightening of her intimate muscles and decided that she was improving, though she couldn't imagine capturing Clint.

When she was learning to kiss and cuddle, men made the first moves and women kept their hands to themselves. They certainly didn't tell their loves where to place their hands and mouths and what pleased them to the ultimate. There was no making love in the daylight or on the floor or in the kitchen or in a woodland glade.

In rural Oklahoma when she was growing up, a boyfriend of a long time might steal a kiss in a barn or after a social, but—

Flashes of Angie, hot after Clint, caused Lilah to scowl at the huge clamshell in which she kept a collection of pencils and notepads. She realized she had clamped her legs together too tightly and that her buttocks were beginning to resent the exercise, too. Lilah flopped to her stomach and her breasts ached.

Clint had nibbled on her through the sheet and her gown right in broad daylight.

Jeff had never attempted to make love to her until the sweet dark hours of the night.

Lilah groaned and flopped to her back again, unable to bear the pressure against her breasts. She jumped up, found her nude body in the moonlight-drenched, full-length mirror and it occurred to her that she had never looked and studied the intrigues of her own womanhood. While the mole at her left nipple remained unchanged, she had lost her coltish look, her body had taken on full breasts and rounded hips. There was a softness to her thighs and Clint's hard length had pressed— Shaken by her thoughts, Lilah leaped into bed and pulled the sheet high to her chin.

Awash in blurred memories of Jeff's tender conventional lovemaking and whatever made Clint bite her gently through the layers of cloth, Lilah drifted into a fitful sleep.

She dreamed of Big Hair, The Floozy and Missy tossing a multicolor array of "strong-and-durable-and-won't-notice-they're-there" packets into the air and raining them upon Clint's mussed hair. He wore that same rakish, devilish gleam that had infuriated her the previous evening.

Lilah awoke to the sound of her own voice. "It isn't possible. That would never fit into something so small and flat."

A dreamy parade of bananas—probably due to the part of the article on practicing sheathing them with "protection"—plopped back into her mind. Jeff had had an operation to prevent another pregnancy after Olympia's difficult birth. There had been no need to explore protection. But now when abstinence was recommended, women were encouraged to make firm choices. She didn't believe the section of the article about women applying the device to their partner. It was too intimate a task....

She had never touched Jeff intimately in their entire marriage. She had never actually seen him....

Lilah pushed back in her mind the instructions about making love to men. About stating her rules for what she wanted and when, and showing her love and desire—

Desire couldn't possibly run that strong and hot or make a woman melt not just once but again and again. Playful encounters with men of her choice—she realized she would have to love a man to allow the deepest physical bonding—weren't... acceptable.

At exactly four o'clock in the morning, she realized she could no longer remember exactly how Jeff kissed. Or how her husband had felt or weighed upon her, or smelled.

She knew suddenly that their sweet lovemaking had never been prolonged, erotic, inventive or playful. Or earthshaking and explosive.

At five o'clock, Lilah realized that she had never spent the night without a nightgown and now she lay nude between the sheets.

At five-fifteen, she knew that Jeff's lovemaking was dear and caring, but that they had never indulged in swift, indulgent repeat performances within the hour or even in the same night. They'd revered their love, cherished and nourished it at a set, proper hour after dark. A friendly coming-together, Jeff had given himself when it was time for him and she had been glad that she had pleased him.

Lilah pushed away the nagging thought that her own intimate earthshaking climaxes had never actually occurred.

At five-thirty, she hoped that sweet young Missy didn't read magazine guides on how to satisfy men and herself. Lilah hoped Missy wouldn't demonstrate her love and affection for Clint. Lilah remembered her daughter's "nubbin" comment and hoped that Clint had not personally tucked Missy into bed.

At five forty-five, she decided to get dressed and scrub the kitchen floor and clean out her spice rack. Then she decided to dust and vacuum and polish the leaves of her new lemon tree on the patio. It seemed vastly unfair that women who loved in the present had all the advantages of rockets and stars while making love.

When the last leaf gleamed in a waxy texture, Lilah knew several things. The world had changed and she hadn't. While Clint was her steadfast friend, his life linked with hers, he was also very vulnerable. Magazines and drugstores prepared women far more than they prepared men to deal with sensuality at middle age. Angie, Missy and Clint's past women had all the advantages, leaving Clint at their mercy. Olympia and Rosemary were right—it was no wonder he was so charged up and looking for "earthshaking, sweat-making, body-heating, sweet, breathless kissing and heart-palpitating lovemaking."

Lilah sat in her patio at seven o'clock and knew without a doubt that Clint probably had never been exposed to the techniques extolled by magazine articles and ads. Very few of the women he had dated were deep thinkers and probably allowed him to proceed in the old-fashioned, male-sets-the-rules-and-pace. Clint needed genuine relationships, not "foofy" ones, and he needed to realize that romantic modes had changed. If he was to make a successful plunge out of his loneliness, women's emotions had to be considered. It was up to her to bring him up to date, she decided as she marched up the stairs and lugged her magazines out to her kitchen table.

She picked up a banana from the fruit bowl and considered it. She would talk to Clint about Missy. Then she would do her best to educate him; she'd help him through his midlife crisis and protect him.

Lilah in a hot July Sunday-afternoon snit did things to a man, Clint decided warily as they rode their horses side by side. The winding stream was lined with cool, shady cottonwoods and the meadowlarks trilled in the pasture.

Dressed in jeans and a bright yellow T-shirt, Lilah knew how to ride. She sat in the saddle easily, though she'd explained it had been years since she last rode. The slight breeze caught her hair, lifting the reddish tints away from her face. The tilt of her chin was that of a woman who looked life in the face and met its challenges.

"I hope you made an early night of it last night, Clint," she said tightly without looking at him.

Clint thought of Missy's wounded look when he'd gently pushed her into her house alone.

"She's just twenty-four, Clint. Do your math," Lilah stated, flicking him a wary look. "Rosemary and Olympia are almost the same age and so are your sons.

I never thought you'd be one of those men who wanted to marry someone half his age, then 'bring her up right.' Dating someone much younger is fine, if you know the new rules and treat the women as equals."

"Did you ride all the way out here to nag me?" Clint asked pleasantly, wanting to forget the past for the moment; he wanted to begin anew with Lilah. Her clean looks and strength made him feel lighthearted and that wasn't a feeling he wanted to lose. "I can still beat you to that clearing," he challenged, watching her sizzling stare.

"Eat my dust," she muttered, digging her heels into the mare he had chosen for her.

His gelding could have easily taken her mare, but Clint liked riding beside Lilah, watching her concentrate, her body taut and full and womanly against the wind. A strong woman who had met her tests, Lilah didn't apply cosmetics and she glowed with health now; it was good to see the shadows peeled from her expression. She laughed, a free melody that pleasured him, and her face lit with enjoyment as she looked at him. Clint wanted to ease her onto his horse and hold her close. Then they reached the clearing and he swung down before she left the saddle and raised his arms to her.

His heart gentled and warmed as Lilah allowed him to help her. When she stood in front of him, she winced and started to rub her backside, then stopped when she saw he was watching. "Sore?" he asked as she took a step back and inhaled sharply.

She resumed rubbing her bottom briskly. "I've been exercising. I want to talk with you, Clint. You need my help."

"I do?" he asked, carrying the small thermal picnic basket from his horse. "What kind of exercises? You look pretty fit to me now."

"Just general limbering up and tightening...toning. Never mind." Lilah walked stiffly to the shady cottonwoods and spread the picnic blanket. She looked at the blanket, then at him, then away, a flush rising on her cheeks.

Clint realized suddenly that Lilah was looking at him, at his body—really looking with a shielded, curious wariness. Because that pleased him, he slowly unbuttoned his shirt, took it off and hung it from a limb. "Hot for July," he explained.

"Going to get hotter," Lilah answered in a strained, husky whisper as her eyes widened and locked to his chest. When her gaze moved slowly down him, awareness surged through Clint.

He curled his fingers into his palms. He wouldn't rush her. Neither would he let her retreat from him.

"Just how are you going to help me, Lilah?" he asked as he sat and tugged off his boots. After glancing up at her, his fingers circled her ankle and he pulled off her canvas shoes. Then he sprawled back on the blanket and braced his arms behind his head, looking up at her. Lilah scanned the available space on the blanket as though she were considering a dangerous move to the moon. Clint knew that she was sifting through time—making a choice that was not within her experience. He held his breath while she eased to one corner of the blanket and began to unpack the fried chicken and potato salad. She shifted uncomfortably for several seconds as though her muscles were protesting the saddle.

Clint rolled to his side to eat and tried not to reveal how much Lilah's cautious glances pleased him.

She sat very tense, her legs curled beneath her, as they discussed crops, the tractor business and Old Sam's arthritis and Mrs. Wilks's insufficient pension. Then Lilah packed away the remainder of the lunch and leaned against the tree; she looked at the slow-moving creek. Because Clint wanted her with him and not longing for the past, he placed his head in her lap and gently moved her hand over his heart, which was beating for her.

He wondered when he hadn't longed for her in the last four years. . . .

"You can't go on like this, Clint. I won't let you," Lilah was saying softly. "I have chosen to prepare and protect you and ease your passage through this difficult time. It's the least I can do. Then when you're in a more logical mood, you'll be better prepared to deal with your—ah . . . your needs and sort them out properly. If you get carried away with Missy and get married, with your old-fashioned ideas, you could have problems later on. Things have changed drastically since you and I were—were learning how to date. I wouldn't want you hurt because you don't know what's new in dating or the relationships between men and women."

"For instance?"

She shifted restlessly. "Well, for instance, women can say things now that they didn't say years ago. And they can do things—personal things—just the same as a man.... Of course, I don't think morals have changed that much—I mean, I really think that marriage is the ultimate bond a man and woman can achieve and that abstinence is best until—ah, just that one special person who you know you are already married to in your heart—I mean...uh...if a man did do those things to a woman...ah, that's not saying that..."

Clint held very still. Then while Lilah was floundering and looking confused in her best Joan-of-Arc-at-the-stake, he nuzzled her soft stomach. The tender weight of her breasts quivered upon him. "Don't get too comfortable and go to sleep, Clint. I'm all wound up to have my say," she muttered. "If you're set to marry or cull a woman for a lifetime relationship, you'd better listen."

"Good enough," he murmured, his thumb stroking her wrist. He noted that her fingertips were softly prowling through the hair on his chest as she formed her thoughts.

"Sure is hot," Lilah stated airily a moment later. "Remember when we used to swim in this creek?"

"Yep," he agreed, angling his arm and free hand higher to caress Lilah's back. While she was considering the heat, Clint gently applied pressure to ease her breasts against his face.

Lilah stilled. He kissed the exact tip of each soft round weight. Her fingers curled into the hair on his chest and he sensed the tenseness humming through her. But she didn't move away and he grinned up at her.

"You'd be mortified if I did that to you, Clint Danner," she stated darkly. "And that's your whole problem. You don't know what a modern woman is prepared to do to a man. If I kissed you there—"

"Try it," he challenged, narrowing his eyes at her.

"Don't you dare me. After spreading yourself over me and mashing me to the mattress, it would serve you right to be mashed in turn."

He continued to look up at her and Lilah flushed. If she backed away now— "Okay, you deserve this," she said resolutely, moving away from him. She crouched beside him, looking very heated, tousled and determined. "This is one lesson you need."

"I'm waiting," Clint said, realizing that every nerve in his body might explode if Lilah put her lips on his body.

She inhaled and began looking down at his chest. "I am not experimenting, Clint Danner. So don't think I'm man-hungry. I'm just doing this for your own good and to prove a point."

If he got any hotter or tauter waiting for her—

Lilah timidly touched his nipple with her fingertip and Clint almost jerked her beneath him. But he forced himself to lie rigidly waiting. "Well?" he managed to say huskily.

"I want to know just who has kissed you there, Clint Danner," Lilah said firmly, gently touching each nipple. "Did Big Hair Pilar? Or Angie? Or poor sweet Missy?"

"Poor sweet Missy" had tried to unzip his jeans the moment they got into his pickup. Her experienced hands had been all over him before he'd caught them.

"Not any woman," he stated evenly, meaning it.

Lilah's eyebrows lifted and she smirked as though she'd won a major victory. "You see, Clint. You're not up-to-date. Women do different things now— They have equal rights and they can set the pace, and..." Lilah's honey brown eyes darkened as she stared at his chest, then his thighs. She frowned when she considered the area of his zipper as though troubled about a distant problem.

Then, taking a last you-asked-for-it look at him, Lilah slowly bent to suckle his left nipple.

Shock waves rippled through Clint. Her untutored lips closed again and her tongue flicked him gently. "Lilah!" Clint heard himself explode and realized that he'd been holding his breath overlong.

"Women are participants now," she affirmed, pressing her hands down on him to tether him. When she kissed his right nipple, Clint sucked in his breath and closed his eyes, his body rock-hard and poised to—

He jackknifed into a sitting position, glared at Lilah, then stood and ran toward the creek. He dived into the swirling water and let it cool the emotions surging through him before he would allow himself to tangle with Lilah again. When he surfaced, she was scanning the water, her expression concerned. "You are a strange man, Clint Danner," she said thoughtfully. "Taking a swim in the middle of a serious discussion about your out-of-date viewpoint on men and women's relationships isn't normal."

Clint grabbed a fallen limb and surged out of the water to stand beside her. "In," he ordered darkly and took a step toward her. She had pushed him to the limits and stood there looking innocent while he was dealing with— "In," he repeated.

"I'm not in the mood to go swimming. I don't even have my swimsuit— Clint!" Lilah sank beneath the water where Clint had tossed her. She surfaced, shook the hair from her eyes and glared at him. "You see? Missy wouldn't stand a chance with you. You're too excitable. You don't know anything at all about pacing. I've shocked you. You're so used to having your way... You don't understand pacing or—"

Clint dived into the water and surfaced beside her. He pushed her head beneath the water and when Lilah came up, she began splashing him.

"Hey! Dunk me, will you?" She laughed and began kicking water in his face.

Clint dived, swam under Lilah and stood with her sitting on his shoulders. Lilah laughed again, a carefree sound, and wrapped her arms around his neck. "If I go under, you do, too."

"You should know better than to threaten me, Lilah," he stated before sinking to the bottom of the creek.

"This is silly," Lilah said a few minutes later as they floated lazily in the water. But when she grinned at him, Clint knew she wasn't thinking about the past; she was enjoying the present.

"Tell me about some of these new rules," he invited, appreciating the way her wet T-shirt clung to her breasts.

Lilah treaded water and allowed his feet to anchor hers as they floated. "You were shocked just a moment ago, Clint. Making changes won't be easy for you," she said thoughtfully. "You could be too set in your ways. You aren't that young anymore, neither am I."

Clint looked at her across the water. "You know what, Lilah McCord? Sometimes you're just plain old gloomy."

"*I* realize my age," she stated righteously.

"You kiss like you did when you were twelve years old," he returned. "Haven't learned a thing despite your grand advanced-and-worldly age."

She glared at him. "Not everyone has been culling an entire countryside in the past few years," she said meaningfully. "You can't just go hunting for love."

Clint blew a stream of water in the air and floated by her side, looking up at the fading sunlight dappling the cottonwoods. His shoulder bumped hers companionably in the cool water. "What are the new rules for kissing? Can a person breathe or not?"

He laughed when Lilah shot him a withering glare, then trudged to the bank and tried to pull herself out of the water. He surged up to the bank and lowered his hands to help her. Lilah looked up at him grimly, then nodded. Clint scooped his hands under her arms and pressed the gentle swell of her breasts as he lifted her to stand in front of him. He kept one hand where it was on her wet body, and with the other pushed away her hair from her face.

Lilah's hands stayed where she had gripped his shoulders, her nails digging slightly into his bare skin. Her eyes were shadowed, dark with questions, hesitation, fears and mystery, and Clint leaned slowly down to place his mouth over hers. Lilah stood very still as he changed the angle of the kiss, deepening it.

Testing her and himself, Clint let the tip of his tongue drift along her soft lips, licking the drops and tasting her. Lilah's fingers dug gently into his shoulders and she moved closer against him, shivering just once.

The heat deep within her quivered and stirred—

When he kissed the droplets of water clinging to her lashes, she inhaled and trembled, her mouth parting slightly. With a flush touching her cheeks, her eyes looking up at him in a sexy, drowsy stare and her lips parted and waiting, Clint sensed her hunger and eased his hand under her wet T-shirt and bra.

Lilah went rigid, her eyes widening slightly and her breath coming rapidly as he gently caressed the full, swelling softness. "Can I taste you, honey?" Clint asked and realized how he could frighten her back into the safety of the past.

"Yes," she whispered unevenly. "Oh, Clint... I'm aching, Clint."

Taking care to move very slowly, Clint drew her down to the blanket. Lilah clung to his shoulders as he moved over her. "I don't believe I'm doing this," she whispered when he finished kissing her.

Clint sensed that she trusted him and he cherished the gift, pushing away his sharp hunger to see her, to taste her—

Very gently, Clint removed her T-shirt and bra and Lilah quickly crossed her arms over her breasts. "We're lying here in broad daylight, Clint. What if someone comes along?" she asked desperately.

"The horses will let us know soon enough." He looked down at her breasts and slowly moved away her hands to lace his fingers with hers. "Let me look at you."

"Clint," she whispered in a tone that caught him. "I do ache so, Clint."

She tasted sweet and womanly and fresh. Clint felt her fingers run through his hair, holding him tight against her. Her cry lifted high into the cottonwoods and sailed away and her body trembled beneath his.

"Oh, my!" she exclaimed as he lowered his chest to her and eased her knees high along his waist. He kissed her again, letting her know the heat ruling him, the desire that had ridden him for her for years, and pressed down firmly on her hips.

Lilah cried out again, moving restlessly beneath him. "Clint...I think I'm going to burst," she whispered as he braced his arms beside her and suckled her breasts. Then, unable to stop, Clint ran his hands under her soft, wet denim-covered hips and lifted her boldly against him.

Lilah's fingers found his chest and she looked up at him, frowning. "I want to talk about this," she stated very tightly.

Clint closed his eyes and realized that the droplets on his forehead weren't all from their swim. He caressed the twin softnesses in his palms, luxuriating in her full curves. Her intimate heat burned him through the layers of wet clothing— Clint shivered as he realized that Lilah was flexing her muscles. Her buttocks contracted and released in the cup of his hands.

She studied his expression while continuing her movements and Clint frowned down at her. "What are you doing?"

"Exercising. I've let myself go to pot. Well...I didn't actually know about doing exercises to firm and tighten and control passion—"

She pursed her lips thoughtfully then looked up at him with concern. "Do you think that people actually do all those things, Clint? I mean, twist and—" Lilah eased her knees higher, and but for the cloth separating them, he would have sunken deeply into her.

"Do you know that women have—" Lilah swallowed and gripped his wrists as if he were her lifeline to another world. She concentrated on keeping his hips locked between her knees as though she had him trapped and wasn't letting him go until she had her answers. "Do you realize that women have...have a spot that when...that can...ah...make her very hot? Did you know that, Clint? I didn't and I was married for years. To be truthful, I can't say that I've ever...ever seen stars or exploded," she whispered worriedly.

Clint heard himself groan and glanced down to see her breasts quiver as she continued her tensing and relaxing movements. She smoothed away the water clinging to the hair on his chest and studied it intently. "You're a good friend and you probably won't understand this, Clint. But I've decided to give Edward Jamison another chance."

"You do and I'll spank your behind," Clint stated flatly and hoped that he wouldn't embarrass them both in the next few seconds. "Stop moving like that."

"Spanking is passé," she returned, outraged. "Today's woman would never stand for it. Women want relationships, partnerships and equality in all things, including sex. They want to be participants in relationships. While men usually want space, women want intimacy—"

"Then I'll do something just as effective," he threatened.

"Clint. I'm going to tell you something that will make you better understand my position. I've just decided it, because I don't want to be as out-of-date as you are. I think you should know that I've never had an climax—yes, don't look so shocked, Mr. Know-It-All.

That is what the ultimate experience is called in all the magazines, a climax orgasm.''

She paused and then asked in a tone of discovery and wonder, ''Clint, did you know that it can happen several times? I had no idea. I didn't even know that with one touch in the right place, a man can—''

When he ripped himself away to lie rigidly beside her, looking up at the clear blue sky and wondering what had just run over him, Lilah raised herself to one elbow and looked down at him worriedly. ''I don't want to talk about anything that has to do with sex now,'' he asserted, avoiding the sight of her breasts near him.

He turned on his side away from her, giving her time to dress before he told her what he thought about— whatever she was just saying.

He'd intended to slowly bring her into the present. To stir her a little, woo her gently and gradually accustom her to the loving that would come naturally between them.... When they were married—

Lilah lay at his back and yawned. She smoothed his tense back and stroked his hair. ''Poor old Clint. I've shocked you. I know I have. You're dear and you're old-fashioned.''

Her fingers tensed on his shoulder. ''But Clint, so help me, I've decided that I want that ultimate experience just once before I get much older. I want a climax,'' she stated firmly.

''We're leaving,'' he stated unevenly as he bent and jerked on his boots. He had to have time to think about the new turn of events in his courting of Lilah.

"It's my choice, Clint," she said, meeting his eyes with her darkened honey-shaded ones. "There's no reason we can't act like adults and continue our friendship."

"Exactly what are you going to do to Jamison?" Clint demanded when they were mounted and his eyes wouldn't leave the twin points pushing against Lilah's wet clothing. "Zap him?"

"Test him. See if he's a cull," she answered honestly. "I see now that you were right about that, though I'm certain you're going about it wrong and with the wrong techniques and the wrong women. I want to call my own tune. To explore my sensuality before it's too late and with a man who is loving and touching and romantic. Though we loved each other—Jeff and I—I realize that my marriage lacked intimacy, a sharing of the deepest boundaries, physical and mental. I see the true value of your dating experiences, Clint, though yours probably weren't of the variety I'm wanting—very slow and sensual and relational and loving. I just didn't realize the process. On the other hand, I don't think that the women you were seeing were into realizing the depths of a relationship like I want to."

Lilah glanced at him. "Don't worry. I think I can explore myself and still take care of you. You're my friend, after all."

"Anything else?" he asked darkly as Lilah raised her arms to the sky and stretched in a feminine arc of curves and sensuality. Riding the horse, her thighs raised higher and catching the rolling rhythm, she looked like a pagan goddess offering herself to love.

"Not just now. I'm going to work on the situation. See who I am and what's new between men and women. I'm not taking this lightly—the discovery that I've fallen so far behind. I want to know everything and I want to find a meaningful relationship. I want to see stars, Clint. I want to know that I love the man who is sharing himself—everything that he is—with me and then I want to explode. Maybe several times if it's really possible. If I have— If I have a significant other or a husband," she said slowly as if tasting the thought, "I want him to be my friend and my lover and my equal. There are times that I might want to be a bit . . . savage . . . dominating . . . strong, and I want a man who can understand my need to— My needs as a now-woman," she finished firmly.

Her gaze darkened and leveled at him. "I have never made love in daylight, or more than once a night."

Clint sat in his saddle, aching, and wondered, who was this woman? He'd sat beside her in church and smelled her sweet, clean scent for years. He'd seen her with her children and his, and nurturing the aged and the despairing. . . . She had been selfless, with the exception of holding her heart from pain. "Explode," he repeated.

"Don't you sit there with your eyebrow cocked high and look disgusted, Clint. Men and women talk about things like that now. Or maybe they just let their bodies do the talking. It's called communicating."

"What was that you said about midlife crisis?" he reminded her.

Lilah studied the Herefords grazing in the field and the oil rigs slowly bobbing up and down. "My theory is that I've just now come into my sensuality.... And that you're behind in this new man-woman relationship business and you have that dominating, male viewpoint that doesn't recognize the empowered woman. In fact, my sensuality—a woman's—will probably last longer than yours. Clint, as much as you've been testing the countryside, there is a possibility that your heater is dimming. You should be aware of...potential...ah...nonperformance problems when a woman takes charge. As your friend, I'll do my best to help you. I want your promise that you won't be marrying Missy and that you'll keep an open mind about all this."

"An open mind," he repeated. "Performance problems."

"Stop repeating everything and scowling at me, Clint. Race you to the fence," she challenged, grinning at him.

4

Mid-July was hot and dry. Lilah read the signals from the town gossips; she knew she had wounded and disgusted Clint Danner.

She'd shocked him with her talk of intimacy in relationships. His temporary condition would pass; Clint would remain her friend and he would better know what a now-woman wanted in a relationship. It would be unfair of him to lurch into marriage or a lifetime relationship without realizing how women's attitudes had changed.

Lilah briskly applied lotion to her arms and legs and wondered where in her apartment she was going to place the new expensive exercise machine. She was forced to consider the excessive energy humming through her, especially when jolts of Clint's lips suckling and tugging on her breasts shot back into her body. Exercise and abstinence seemed a good plan until she could safely balance her new modes.

Abstinence was certainly a commodity that she knew well. Not that she wanted to explore lightly or without commitments—

She really did want to experience the height of her womanly sensuality before it was too late.

Wearing a large hat, a trench coat and sunglasses and lurking around the "prevention" shelves at Potsburg's drugstores was a genuine education. She hoped that Sissy Doolittle hadn't recognized her; Lilah had barely had time to replace the variety of boxes she'd been comparing—the information was truly amazing—and scoot around the corner of the aisle, before Sissy arrived.

Clint had avoided Lilah's Billiards for a solid week and had holed up at his ranch and his tractor business. Sol McMillian said Clint had hot-rodded his tractor; Clint had tossed a too-quiet, temper snit when he was asked to slow the motor. Angie had parked her sports car in front of his store and had crawled under a tractor with him. There had been a quick tangle of her legs with his jeans and the next minute Clint had come scooting out on his roller pad, drenched in dirty oil. Beneath the tractor, Angie had become hysterical and Clint had had to pull her out by her heels. She'd screeched for a good half hour and demanded that Clint take her out to repay his damage. He'd refused, though he'd wavered a bit when she'd cried brokenly. According to Lacy Frank and Tom Feather, Missy was acting just as pouty as Angie.

Lilah realized she had affronted Clint, placing his age and out-of-date problems at his boots. She hadn't wanted to hurt him, but only friends could tell each other something so intimate. She hoped the information was helpful—that Clint would become an up-to-date man because of her attention.

She trusted Clint absolutely. He might not like what she was considering, or what she had implied—rather, flat out told him. But he wouldn't hold it against her, she knew, nor would he discuss the matter with anyone else.

Clint was her friend and she needed someone who understood her now.

If she failed in her new life's adventure, he'd stand by her. He'd see her through the hazards and downfalls the same as he always had and he would protect her.

Protection.

Lilah wondered about Clint and protection. The thought was inconceivable. The dimensions didn't match. He'd probably been thinking about Angie when his jeans had tightened across his lean hips.

Lilah pulled back her couch, making room for her investment, the super-duper, multipurpose exercise machine. She wanted to exercise in the morning, sunlight and fresh air coming through her front window. The multidimension machine would exercise and tone each part of her. Lilah turned on the television, pushed in the video and fast-forwarded it to the section she wanted; she began using the light weights in an exercise to tone her upper "grandma's" arms, then the telephone rang.

Rosemary, with her baby yelling for cookies in the background, was worried about Clint. Lilah assured her daughter that she had faxed Clint and his return fax said he was "Just fine. Never better." Rosemary didn't believe him; something was wrong. "Ask him for a date, Mom. There's no reason you can't find some companionship at your ages. At least it will give you both something to do and you can take care of Clint."

"Ask Clint Danner for a date?" Lilah repeated slowly as she watched the wind ripple through the plants on the patio below her.

"Make it 'sound' like a real date. That way, he'll have to keep it and won't hole up at his ranch, brooding about Angie or Miss Foofy. You've been friends for so long that no one will notice and dressing up and getting out won't hurt you a bit. Now-women can ask guys for dates. It's not taboo any longer, like it was in your day. Have to go.... The baby is headed toward the television."

"A date," Lilah repeated as she replaced the receiver in its cradle. "A date with Clint." She tasted the words and found herself smiling.

On Saturday night, Clint was as edgy and wary as a new bride without the nervous giggles. He was also delectable in a new cotton shirt and slacks and his always-shining boots. Lilah wanted her discovery about equality to start right and had arranged to meet him at the café, rather than either one picking up the other. She had waited for Clint in a back booth and felt energized and toned by the new exercises she had been doing on her machine.

When he arrived, all showered and smelling good, his eyes darkening at the sight of her, she credited the lurching of her heart to her exercise program. The maddening urge to push him down in the booth and run her fingertips through that shining little tuft of chest hair escaping his collar surprised her.

While they were being served and while they were eating, Clint spoke little, but his probing looks were saying plenty—if she just knew what he was thinking. No doubt he was hoping that he wouldn't be wounded or more disgusted than he already was with her. Lilah did not push him, because she knew Clint would get around to what he was thinking soon enough. And she didn't really know if she wanted to hear what he had to say.

Clint took in the tropical print, sarong-style, low-cut dress. "Have you worn that around Jamison?" he demanded, staring intently at her bosom.

She shifted restlessly on the booth seat, slightly uncomfortable with the new lacy, underwire bra that matched her slip and panties. The push-up feature molded her curves higher and needed wearing time to adjust. "I haven't, but that's not saying I won't," she returned easily.

"You jiggle in that get-up," Clint stated baldly. "I can't see your backside, but I hope you've got more on it than on your top part."

"My backside is covered just fine." She inhaled briefly and refused to count to ten. She preferred that he be truthful with her about how she looked—but just not that honest. "Clint, I know that I'm out of shape. I'm working on firming up now. I'm going to be lean and mean. I just got this new thigh exerciser that I can use while I'm watching television. My heartbeat is getting in top-notch fit—"

His strong, big hand latched around her wrist. "Getting fit to explode?" he asked in a meaningful tone that set her nerves on edge.

"Could be.... When I'm ready," she retorted firmly and watched his eyes flicker, something dark and hot moving through his expression. "You don't have to act so uneasy, Clint."

"I should have picked you up at your place. Men collect women on dates, you know."

"Stop growling. You're so standard old-fashioned, Clint. I am determined to be a now-woman."

"A now-woman?" he repeated, looking at the large fuchsia blooms over her chest. His expression, intent and hungry, caused her breasts to swell and harden. She hoped she wouldn't damage the construction of her new underclothing, and that she would not swell over the top of her bodice.

He touched her ring finger, tracing the small indentation caused by her wedding band. "You took off your wedding ring."

Lilah looked at the pale band of flesh on her finger. "He's in my heart, that's enough."

She looked at Clint. "We're locked in the past, you and I. As friends, there is no reason we can't—" She took the café bill from the waitress and lifted her purse.

Clint scowled at her. "What are you doing?"

"Paying. We'll either go Dutch treat, or I'm buying. I did ask you out, you know."

"A woman paying for me? I don't think so," Clint murmured warily. "What would that look like? I'll tell you what—like I was down on my luck or a paid-for stud—"

Lilah rose to her feet and smoothed her dress. Clint's gaze stopped at her waist. "Does that thing really untie with one tug of that bow?" he asked in a raw tone as he slowly rose to loom over her.

"Either you're acting contrary and ornery, or you're wondering about how things fasten," Lilah said, nettled that her first attempt to date wasn't going smoothly, due to one Clint Danner. He smelled and looked supremely good tonight—despite his reference to her out-of-shape, soft, jiggling body.

His smoky blue gaze strolled down to the short hem and her high heels. "You usually wear long skirts to church that swish when you walk. If the wind is right, they look flirty. There's not enough material in that skirt to blow. That's a whole lot of long legs for one woman to be showing."

Because he seemed so shaken, Lilah allowed her thigh to press against the sarong slit and it parted gently to reveal her leg. She pointed the toe of her strapped high-heel shoe and the light glistened on her newly painted-and-shaped toenails. Daring Clint and watching his reactions was fascinating. "What do you think about this style?"

He sucked in air and looked behind her at the painting of Texas longhorns on a hot, dusty trail drive. She thought she heard him mutter, "I hope I last through this."

"What did you say?"

"It's hot... been a long, dry spell."

"July usually is," she returned and didn't understand the sudden grim look he shot at her.

Clint looked very uncomfortable while Lilah paid, and because he looked so bruised and disgusted as he jammed his hat on his head, she took his hand in hers as they walked down the street.

There was a good sense of eternity, walking down this beloved street with her lifetime friend. His fingers laced with her smaller ones, and whatever had been driving her since she'd found that she wasn't a now-woman, eased and warmed. Clint's presence could be comforting and dearly familiar, when he wasn't "culling them," or riling her. His thumb gently rubbed the back of her hand and she allowed peace to wash over her.

Her peaceful mood lasted until Clint ordered tightly, "Don't wear that dress with any one else."

Lilah stopped beside his pickup, which sat in the café's secluded parking lot. Night had draped like silk over Green Tomato and stars spread across the sky. "You're not walking me home, Clint. And since this is the only dress I've got for now-woman dating, I may have to wear it again."

"What's the plan, Lilah?" Clint asked warily as she opened his truck's door on the driver's side.

She moved close to him, lifted her arms to his neck and stroked the hair at his nape. All this could prove to be too much for old-fashioned Clint; she intended to be firm, but gentle. "I'm going to kiss you and send you home."

He snorted in disbelief—until she backed him against the driver's seat and pulled his head down to hers.

He tasted hungry and male, laced with a humming anticipation that she feared slightly, though she trusted him. She trusted him even as he changed the kiss, reaching down to cup her bottom and lift her higher. She noted that Clint's big hands knew how to cup and exactly where.

The pickup's bench seat creaked as Clint eased backward and pulled Lilah into the cab. His groan was edged with frustration and the excitement of it went soaring through Lilah. "Open your mouth, Clint," she ordered softly, her fingers spearing through his hair.

Lying beneath her on the pickup seat, his hair mussed and his eyes dark and gleaming in the shadows, Clint inhaled. His big hands caressed her back. "Little girl, you could get into big trouble—"

"Not with you," she stated firmly and slowly lowered her mouth to his. Clint held very still while she tested positions of her lips against his. He sucked in his breath when she slid the tip of her tongue gently across his bottom lip and eased into his mouth. Clint groaned slightly and gently suckled her tongue.

A storm of emotions washed over her and she framed his hard cheeks with her hands. Lilah tried nibbling his lips, flicking them with her tongue, and held him still when he tried to escape her.

Holding Clint beneath her evoked a new excitement that Lilah had never thought possible.

He could easily displace her.

He could easily seal his lips from hers, or with a word tell her that he was frightened of her.

He could say no and she'd still respect him.

"I truly appreciate this, Clint," she whispered against his lips and then tried her best to form a heat-making kiss, complete with nibbles and bites.

Clint stiffened beneath her and raised slightly. "You bit me, Lilah McCord," he said unevenly.

"Did I hurt you?" she asked immediately, concerned that she had gone too far on poor old Clint and he wasn't up to the heady thrill the kiss was intended to create—at least according to the magazine's guide to sensual kissing.

"Hell, no. Surprised me, though," he admitted, staring up at her. He slowly lay down on the seat and Lilah rested upon him, reassured by his strength and the companionable silence as they looked at each other.

"You're hard," she said finally, meaning that he was all angles and muscles to her softness. She squirmed on him to get more comfortable. "But then, I'm really out of shape. I'm working on that."

"I am very hard," he stated rawly as his hand smoothed the back of her thighs, tracing the black lace garter down to her hose. He slipped his fingertips into the hose, smoothed her skin, then eased them back up to the lace of her panties. "You know, I think I've heard about that A or B or whatever spot idea...."

Lilah held very still while Clint's fingertips moved between them. "Do you really think that's true?" she asked, trembling and clenching her thighs tightly.

"Just could be." Clint watched her as her eyes widened and she gripped his shoulders for a lifeline.

"I trust you, Clint. Touch me. I want to see if that's true."

He stared up at her, frowning darkly. She realized she had gone too far and Clint was frightened of her.

"Hell, no," he said for the second time, looking at her bodice. His face looked flushed and strained. "That isn't a thing you do in a back parking lot of Green Tomato."

"Oh." Lilah looked down at Clint and realized that she was not releasing him just yet. "We're in the *deserted, shadowed, concealed* parking lot. Hidden in the alley and protected by trees and signs," she argued and hoped it didn't sound as if she was pleading with him.

"It's a private thing, Lilah," he returned in a flat, sharp tone. "I've heard that women might call out—"

"Not me. I never have, anyway."

"Uh-huh. I don't think I want to know the details," he muttered.

She exalted in her newfound discovery, the delight in trapping a man she respected, trusted and liked beneath her. She angled her legs along his, testing the length of his to hers and wondered if she should do what she wanted just then. "I'm probably ruining that spit-shine you have on your boots."

"Do it, Lilah," Clint ordered tightly, his hands locking firmly to her bottom. "Whatever it is that's causing you to think and frown and wonder...don't worry about my spit-shine—just do it."

"I was wondering if you—if men call out or what they think about women doing the same—at the height—I mean, when the exploding begins— And just how long...?"

Clint looked stunned, then disgusted with her. "Never knew anyone who used a stopwatch when— Could we talk about something else?" he asked, moving restlessly beneath her.

"Okay," she answered, then asked the question that had dominated most of her thoughts since she'd read that article about bananas. "Clint, has a woman ever placed protection on you? Is that really possible? I mean—is it painful?"

Clint blinked, shook his head as though to clear it and stared at her as though he'd never known her. Then his expression shifted, darkened and narrowed like a Westerner sighting his prey. Clint's expression wasn't harsh, but rather alert and very thoughtful. He studied her face, and a miniature lightning storm seemed to quiver between them. She flushed until his hand moved gently to cup her breast. She concentrated on the friendly, erotic, lazy caress and something within her settled and warmed. She liked it very much—at least when Clint was the man holding her. Then he said softly, "Some men might like a little noise. Quiet is good, too."

"But what about you?" she pressed, excited now that he seemed more receptive to her questions. Clint had developed new, interesting facets, ones she wanted to explore. She inhaled when his fingers ran over the tip of her breast, hardening it.

"Can't remember. Really can't remember any past loving now, Lilah. I've been too busy concentrating on—"

"I...ah...seem to be very sensitive there. It could be the construction of my new underwear," Lilah managed to say as Clint eased her lace aside to gently kiss her upper breast.

"I like it," he whispered in a deep, husky tone. Then he smoothed the material back in place and she was left with an unsettled sense of expectancy for something marvelous that had not occurred.

She wanted to rip his shirt aside and place her breasts to his, nipple to nipple.

He'd be too shocked. She'd set him back light-years in his midlife crisis. She had to protect him, and from herself because right now, she did not truly understand her needs. "You're a good friend," she said very gently as she lay down upon him and felt his arms close around her. Clint nuzzled her hair and stroked her back and she sighed. "Thank you, Clint. I needed this."

She held him tighter, because as a new now-woman she wanted to do her share and Clint did need cuddling. She hoped she'd kept him from being too lonely tonight or from missing Angie or Missy.

"My pleasure, Lilah," he returned in the gallant western cowboy phrase that equaled, "You're mighty welcome, ma'am."

Two days later, Clint frowned at the ruined oil pan while Old Sam and Ole discussed Lilah's strange, erratic behavior. Leslie Ford had seen Lilah, dressed in spandex and joggers, running up and down her stairs at about the time people were usually eating supper and doing dishes. Murphy Adams had almost "de-manned" John Many Wings with his pool cue when Lilah had gone zipping by in her new spandex outfit on her way to the cash register.

The shipping delivery van had pulled up to her back door, and Henry Lord told Clint he'd helped the driver lug a heavy box upstairs to her apartment. Lilah had borrowed a wrench from Clint on that same day and had returned for other hardware. She'd kissed his cheek and patted it and stated that people needed to touch more, to get more in tune with their feelings and to show affection for others.

For a half hour after each of her visits, Clint had sat in his office and stared at the wall, wondering what had hit him.

According to Tad, Rosemary's husband, "the mother-in-law and the wife" went to Potsburg to shop and get something done at the beauty shop that they couldn't get done in Green Tomato. Had to do with waxing and makeovers, opening up eye areas by defining eyebrows and the "now-woman"—whatever that was. "They're tanning parts of them that have never seen sunlight before," Tad said with an air of excitement.

Clint knew exactly what Tad was experiencing. Lilah's affection and questions on the seat of his pickup had left Clint in hard, taut agony. He'd been taking cold showers on a regular basis.

Very little tethered him from returning to her apartment and showing her everything she wanted to know, and a little more.

But Lilah McCord was a woman who did things when she knew it was time to do them—like leaving his lap after the funeral and taking her life in hand.

Clint wiped the oil from his hands as a page began to slip from his facsimile machine. Lilah's handwriting curled across it. "Come over tonight, if you're free. About eight. We'll have dinner here."

"Thanks. I'll be there. Want me to bring anything?" he wrote on the note and slid it into the machine.

An hour later, Lilah's handwriting appeared on the page sliding out of the fax machine. "Sorry. May Brittain's cue stick hit Eliza in the eye. She's okay. Bring yourself. L."

That evening, Clint slowly walked up Lilah's outer back stairway. He had a heavy sense of his mortality and his dampered needs threatened to bolt at the first sight of Lilah's fabled spandex. Under her porch light, he glanced down at the slight marks on the toes of his boots; he'd left them as a trophy-reminder that Lilah's kissing him wasn't a dream. Clint slowly took off his hat and prayed that his will—or rather his won'ts were as strong as his desire to have Lilah in a loving, long-term relationship.

The wind slid softly through the dusk and Clint started, uneasy as his light clothing rippled gently down his body. His daughter-in-law had sent him the "get-up" earlier in the summer and he'd pushed the box to the back of the closet.

He hoped his daughter-in-law's famed fashion taste would not make Lilah tease him.

He wasn't in the mood for teasing. A man's clothing shouldn't shift like a snake on his body. Denim did what it should; his jeans were durable, didn't wrinkle if he took them out of the dryer fast enough and smoothed them over the back of the couch. Denim wore like steel. Cotton and denim—they were bred into him; they were his style. This getup would cause talk if he took it to the dry cleaners, because no one brought anything there but treasured pioneer quilts, winter coats and suits.

Lilah had unnerved him. He wanted to grab her with both hands and— But he wouldn't. He'd waited and longed and hungered and he was going with her mood, whatever it was.

Because Jamison and the rest weren't stepping in now, just when Lilah was wondering about intimacy and body spots and relationships with a genuine living man. He intended to be that man, even if he had to wear loose, pleated pants with a narrow belt.

He ran his fingers across his stomach and truly missed his western, tooled leather belt. A leather belt gave a man something to hook his thumbs into securely; and then he knew that everything was as it should be.

The tiny print on his shirt shifted as the breeze rippled through it and Clint shivered. He hoped that no one had seen him as he walked from his pickup to Lilah's patio. He firmly gripped the small sack in his hand and knocked at the door. If he waited much longer, his clothes would scare him further.

Lilah opened the door and her eyes lit at the sight of him. Dreamy music with violins and without a strong beat and words swirled out into the night and wrapped around him. "Clint, you look wonderful. Come in."

She tugged him inside and took his hat. "You look terrific," she exclaimed, pulling him into the middle of her living room and walking around him, studying him. He glanced at the darkened room and at the lit candles on the dining table. He preferred to eat in a well-lighted room, but for Lilah— "Why, Clint. You are making a real fashion statement. I'm impressed," she said with delight as she inspected him from head to toe.

Clint clutched the tiny sack in his hand as she smoothed the nape of his neck, his shoulders and the length of his back. He sensed her hesitation as her touch lingered past his waist.

When Lilah came around to stand in front of him, Clint noted her hair. It had been pushed up high on her head and tiny tendrils escaped at her ears and at the nape of her neck. A slender gold chain circled Lilah's neck and her tight, short, sleeveless black dress gave way to long, bare legs and feet. Another chain circled her ankle. He had hard, sharp images of removing it with his teeth as she wiggled her bare feet. "Clint, I had my first pedicure. It was wonderful."

"What did you do to your face?" he asked slowly, not wanting to offend her, but this Lilah looked vibrant and girlish.

Lilah grinned up at him. He wanted to scoop her against him and tousle that carefully mussed hairdo. "I'm trying new things. I had a makeover and they matched my cosmetics."

She studied his shirt and reached to unbutton the top button. "I am so pleased with you, Clint. Only a friend would know how much this meant to me."

"This stuff wrinkles," he heard himself saying as he tried to force his eyes away from her soft bosom and the deep crevice between her breasts. He cleared his throat and realized that his body was reacting; he moved restlessly and his clothing shifted and settled slowly on him, startling him again. "There's not room enough in that dress for wrinkles."

Lilah pivoted slowly in front of him, modeling the dress. Clint blinked at the image of her curves moving within hands' reach. His head felt light and his body felt heavy— "Do you like it?" she asked, frowning at him. "It's a basic."

"Not much of it," he returned uneasily.

"I know. It feels great. Just wait until I get all toned and lean."

"I like your curves. A man knows where to put his hands and what to lock on to," Clint protested doggedly, then stepped back a foot as he saw the monster lurking in the shadows of the candlelight.

"This is my workout station," Lilah said with delight and dragged him to the huge device of bars and levers and weights. "You can use it with me. Look, you can do leg lifts while I do chest firming."

"Tonight?" Clint asked warily. He had hoped for a romantic evening and advancing in his pursuit to claim Lilah as his own.

Then Lilah was wrapping her arms around him and snuggling to his chest. "Oh, Clint. I really, really appreciate you as my friend," she exclaimed, hugging him tightly.

He caught a whiff of erotic perfume, and a body-heating brush of her breasts and body locked to his and his muscles and instincts went on red alert. He blinked and swallowed and for the first time, really appreciated the light fabric of his getup. Lilah's curves were very close....

He held her a moment longer when she would have moved away and was grateful that she allowed him the privilege. Her body molded with his and Clint heard himself groan into her hair.

Lilah stepped back instantly. "I'm so glad you're learning how to hug. I hope you're hungry. I'm trying something new—a lobster dinner. I've never cooked lobster before—I hope it tastes good."

She glanced warily up at him as his finger followed a tendril down her throat. He sensed she was forming another mind-boggling question. "I wanted to try raw oysters on the half shell. They're supposed to be ... ah ... enhancing. Do you think that's true, Clint?"

"I've heard that same thing," he said, offering the tiny sack to her. When it came to Lilah, he didn't need enhancements.

"Oh, you shouldn't have," she gushed with delight and Clint knew that he would do anything to keep that excitement and pure happiness in her voice. "A beautiful, magnificent shell," she said, grinning up at him. "You're the very first person to give me a seashell, Clint. Oh, look. It's pearly pink on the inside— Thank you," she murmured in a sudden burst of shyness.

"I'm told that kisses make great thank-yous," Clint offered huskily as his hand curved around her throat.

Lilah shivered and stepped back, frowning. "Ah ... not now."

Her fingers gripped the white ruffled shell tightly. "I have a schedule to keep and ... ah ... dinner is waiting."

5

——▶◀——

Lilah settled on the couch near Clint. The short black dress inched higher as she squirmed, aware of his gaze locked to her thighs. She stopped her hands from tugging down the hem; he seemed to enjoy looking at her and really appreciated her efforts to be a now-woman.

However, she didn't know if good old Clint, her friend, was prepared to understand her next step in his education as a now-man; he could be contrary and ill-tempered. She glanced at him cautiously and found him examining her bodice. His dark look into her eyes started her tingling from head to foot. Then he looked at her mouth and her heart skipped a beat. "Let's try one of those kisses," he invited again in a raspy, soft tone that caused her to shiver.

"I don't want to be distracted," she muttered as she picked up the remote control to the video player and punched a button. "Now, Clint. I want you to keep an open mind about this. It's just a thought, and as your friend, I think it might be an overlooked opportunity for you. A broadening opportunity."

He played with the tiny curl at the nape of her neck and studied the shifting tints under the dim light. His hand, callused and familiar, was warm as he stroked her neck and toyed with the tiny gold chain. He sounded distracted and she wanted his full attention. "Mmm."

"You've got to get out of the Angie-and-Missy bog, Clint," Lilah stated firmly.

"Mmm. You smell good," he murmured, wrapping his arm around her shoulders and drawing her closer. Off balance, she placed her hand on his thigh to brace herself and caught the muscles leaping and tensing beneath the smooth fabric.

She wanted to straddle him and make him her love slave— Of course, that flighty impulse was contrary to balancing the relationship she wanted as a now-woman. There was no way big, tough, seasoned Clint Danner would be anyone's "boy toy."

"It's ylang-ylang oil. I took my first candlelit oil-scented bath tonight," she stated, shaken with her thoughts about Clint. "But I think I'm getting a shower massager to get the extra sensations on my skin. I seem to be taking a lot of showers lately as my sensuality— I've been learning how to exfoliate my skin and about the wonders of a loofah sponge. You see, a now-woman can be a businesswoman and fit and up on world issues and fashion, and she can also be very feminine."

She paused in the middle of her proclamation about women camping and roughing it and remaining feminine and now-women.

She wondered if Clint would fit into her shower-bath. He would look better than the men on the television ads for soap. She imagined the soap bubbles clustering and sliding gently down his wet-slick body. Although, if Missy snared him...

Lilah had never seen a man in the daylight in the "all-together."

She badly wanted to see Clint.

But then he just might want to see her—to be equal and fair—and she wasn't all that lean and tight yet. Parts of her would never be coltish and pert and high again.

Clint reached down to lift her thigh-tightener device. He studied the tension on it and pushed it together with his strong hands.

Lilah blinked, aghast as a mental image of Clint's hard, dark body—well, maybe his legs weren't dark, maybe they were lighter... Definitely they were hard. She'd felt them leap at her light touch. Clint was a very hard man.

With soapy body gel flowing down his body, the shower beating over their heads, enclosing them in a steamy—

Lilah swallowed. "Them," she repeated mentally and realized she had just imagined her softer, mature body moving against Clint's. Her hand moved to her throat, concealing her racing pulse and she forced herself to breathe slowly.

She stared at him and was thoroughly shocked to realize in that heartbeat that people actually could make love in places other than in a bed.

Every muscle in her body tightened, including her newly discovered intimate ones as a new tidbit flashed by her: she had never made love vertically.

It couldn't work; the gravity was wrong.

Yet Clint looked as though he could support her either way—if he wasn't too embarrassed. He grimly replaced the thigh tightener to the floor, a flush coming and going in his cheeks.

Lilah stared at Clint and he looked back at her. She realized she had just licked her lips as though savoring a fine gourmet dish.

He frowned, his expression wary. "Now what are you thinking?"

"That showers are great," she returned airily, shocked that she had just remembered that she had never taken a bath or a shower with Jeff. She shielded her blush by glancing at her newly purchased Georgia O'Keeffe picture; her blush heated more until she forced her eyes to her seashell collection.

"Uh-huh," Clint agreed warily. He sounded unconvinced that she had truthfully shared her thoughts and Lilah pushed the play button on her VCR to distract him.

He looked at the woman speaking from the television screen and his fingers tightened slightly on Lilah's neck. "...Nelda Birmingham. I'm thirty-five and have been married and divorced. I'm five foot five and weigh one hundred and five pounds. I like to cook and read and listen to Bach. I would love to meet a man who would someday like to go scuba diving and drive a reindeer sled across Iceland."

Clint scowled at Lilah. She'd invested several hours culling these videotapes of women and she was determined not to be waylaid by his sudden attempt to frost the entire apartment. She slid another tape into the video player. "...Lily Crawford. I'm forty and have never been married, but I do want children, just as many as I can have and as soon as possible. I'm willing to move anywhere, including overseas. I speak fourteen languages fluently, am an heiress and love chocolate. If you are interested, yet are incapable of producing children, artificial methods are acceptable...anything enlarged, sculpted or artificial is acceptable."

The woman on the screen, clearly very wealthy, smiled slyly. "For your part, all that I ask is that you be happy. I'll take care of you."

Clint turned slowly to Lilah as she settled down beside him and a third tape began playing. He shook his head slowly and his jaw had a mulish set to it. "No," he muttered tightly, the word dropping like a rock between them.

"Keep an open mind about this, Clint. Then we'll look at the ones that interest me," she said briskly, refusing to let her new ideas be smashed by his dark steamy look.

His eyebrows shot high in surprise. "You? Men that interest you?"

He was stunned and she had to allow him time to adjust to the idea of dating women outside his previous stereotypes. Lilah patted his knee. "Think of it as an adventure in living—meeting new people, the excitement of hunting for a perfect relationship. Or love. We're not too old to look for new loves, Clint."

Clint chewed on the notion while the third woman spoke of wanting to parasail, ski and snorkle. She enjoyed fine wines and older, experienced men. Or very young and inexperienced. She was a masseuse and promised one free massage session and an herbal body wrap on the first date.

"She's not getting her paws on me," Clint muttered and folded his arms across his chest. Because he seemed so moody, glaring at the television, Lilah removed his boots to make him more comfortable. She slipped a glass of wine into his hand, propped his feet onto her coffee table and hoped that he wasn't totally blocking out the merits of choosing a now-woman. The next tape was of a woman who was at her best and inspired to garden while she was nude and the moon was high—she was looking for a "Greek Adonis" interested in playing "Druid games."

Another sleek businesswoman-type wanted to investigate the pyramids, making love on a camel, and another was a sportswoman, looking for a mate who could keep up with her "athletic endeavors."

"What do you think, Clint?" she asked lightly as he stared at her.

"Pure old horse hooey, is what I think," he stated flatly.

She inhaled and counted to ten, while he watched with interest and toyed with the tiny beads that skimmed from her earlobe. She'd chosen those beads because of their dancing life and sensual brush against her skin—she was glad he seemed fascinated with them. Big Hair and Angie had chosen clunky, bold jewelry, which suited them; she had been afraid that Clint would say something negative about the delicate earrings, ankle bracelet and necklace she had chosen. She didn't want negativity about her attempts to discover herself as a now-woman. "I'll show you the ones I'm thinking about myself," she said, scooting from the couch to insert another tape.

Clint sat very still as the six tapes played of men she had chosen. His dark mood swirled around the dimly lit room, and when the last tape was done, Lilah sat on the opposite end of the couch and watched him carefully. His silence—he had stopped muttering—and the way the muscles clenched ominously in his jaw were not going to deter her. She knew she had to defend her position, then perhaps he would be more receptive to the women on the videos. "I want to explore myself and intimacy, Clint. I want a man who will be my partner and—"

"I'll do it," he said grimly, his face tense.

"Do what? Date those women? Which ones?" she asked with an excitement that now seemed flat and empty. Horror raced through her as she thought about Clint making love to a now-woman on top of an Egyptian pyramid. He could roll and bounce down to his death. Or he could become so entangled in his escapades that he would forget their longtime friendship, discarding it like a dusty old pair of boots.

Clint rose slowly, ran his fingers through his hair and glanced down at her. "I'd like another glass of wine before we get into this. Where is it?"

He pushed her shoulder down when she would have risen. "In the kitchen," Lilah said. "You see, Clint. You're wanting space to think and I, as a now-woman, want you to share your base thoughts with me. You back away from intimacy and that is something that I want very much. While we're friends and we've shared a past, I want more. I want a running mate, a person who is excited about discovering sexuality together—"

"Uh-huh," he murmured soberly before leaving for the kitchen.

The banana was near the edge of the counter and Clint pushed it back gently while considering Lilah's plot and needs. He glanced at the magazine articles sedately taped to the shady side of the refrigerator. Apparently, women carried their own protection now and cellulite could be lost by flushing with water and eating pasta. Fat-gram information was taped everywhere.

Lilah's daily checklist included meditation, work-outs and cool-downs, moisturing and cleansing, and obscure "K" exercises. A kitchen towel had been thrown over a tray and the edge of a foil packet escaped concealment. Clint poured his wine, sensing that he needed fortification for whatever lay beneath that towel.

He drew the towel away to see a variety of styles and colors of protection—and one ill-placed over another banana. His body went rock-hard, jutting against the light cloth of his slacks. For once, he thought of a use for pleats on a man's pants. Clint quickly drank his wine and replaced the towel.

Not one of those video-men were touching Lilah....

If ever a woman could send him into terror, it was Lilah McCord on a now-woman discovery course. He pivoted and returned to the living room and, on his way, hoped her cute little skirt didn't ride any higher.

"There's no way you're getting into this now-woman stuff and leaving me behind. But I won't be tossed to those women without knowing some of the basics and you seem to be a step ahead of me," he stated as he reentered the living room. "When do we begin?"

The shimmering beads at Lilah's ears quivered as she turned to him. Her eyes widened, then she slowly rose to her feet and walked to him. She touched his cheek and ran her finger over his lips. When he kissed her fingertips, Lilah said very carefully, "Clint, we're discussing more than a friendly adventure. This shouldn't be a casual relationship. It requires commitment. With you, I'd want basic intimacy and I'd want to fill my needs and—"

Clint's throat was very tight as he asked, "You'd want more because we already know each other? Because we're already friends?"

Lilah stroked the fabric over his chest very slowly and Clint's heart stopped beating as she studied the buttons on his shirt. "You're old-fashioned, Clint. A caring, old-fashioned man. You could be shocked beyond recovery. I have needs rising in me that are frightening. It's like I'm eighteen again, but now everything is different for women. We can enjoy and be free and rule what is happening to us. I've just begun to understand myself as a woman. Oh, I'm not saying I should try a world of men, but rather just one special person and develop a relationship that is balanced and interesting and exciting."

She looked up at him uncertainly. "I'm shocked to discover that I have been shielding a certain innate need for savagery— Just a touch of it.... Passion, I suppose it could be called.... Would you understand, Clint? Or would you—"

Clint eased her into his arms and closed his eyes when she snuggled close. "I'm a tough old cowboy, honey. I'll weather anything you can throw at me. Nothing can unlatch me from you, not even you and this new intimacy thing."

"Sure. You say that now, before we start," she whispered as he nuzzled her silky, scented hair. "But what if you leave me when the going gets tough, and when—

Clint, you blushed the other day when we were talking about sexuality... about exploding stars and poetic spots. It won't do for you to shut down when I want to talk about my emotions, or explore adventures in living or command my own life-style. And I want all this to mean something to you and to me. You looked shaken, Clint."

Clint held her tighter and rocked her with his body. "I was surprised and— When do we start?" he asked in the raw tone that revealed his unraveling emotions.

Her fingertips ran across his nipples, seeking and testing them, and again Clint appreciated the light fabric. Lilah looked up at him, her eyes large in her heart-shaped face. "Tell me what you're thinking right now— at this minute."

Clint clamped his lips closed. He wanted to lay her down and hold her close and tell her what was in his heart. But he couldn't—he'd frighten her away. "It's personal."

Lilah frowned. "This isn't the time to play fence post, Clint. As a now-man, you have to reveal your deepest thoughts, or at least part of them to me."

He inhaled, gritted his back teeth and took a plunge into being a now-man relating to a woman he wanted very much to romance and to wed. "Okay. You asked for it. I want to go to bed with you, Lilah McCord, and I want to wake up with you—"

He paused when her eyes widened and she stepped away from him, gripping the back of a rocker for support. "Sex," she whispered disbelievingly. "You and me and sex..."

"Hell, no," he muttered, refusing to back away. "Not sex alone. Romance. A relationship. Long-term stuff. With the gates wide open in this intimacy thing, if that's what you want."

Lilah stared at him, frowning. After a long pause in which his heart rose to his throat and he waited for her to toss him out, or to laugh, Lilah said, "It wouldn't work. Not with you and me."

"Why not?" Fear sliced through him, leaving him cold.

She'd think of Jeff every time she touched him.

She'd think of Betty, and the barriers would always lie between them.

"You're about as movable as granite, that's why," Lilah stated, her frown deepening. "You're not a verbal man, Clint. I can't go off exploring myself and working to understand myself in relation to today's woman while you stay in the same old rut, not sharing yourself and continuing like before. I'm talking about a joint commitment to enrich our lives. Then if it doesn't work, we'll both still have profited and learned and become better people."

Whatever Lilah wanted, he wanted desperately, too. It would damn well work.

His tense muscles relaxed and his heart unclenched. She hadn't been thinking about their past spouses. "I can take anything you can toss at me," he said quietly, meaning it.

"A different diet? Pasta? Lots of veggies and fruits?" she asked, her eyes beginning to sparkle.

"No problem."

"Exercise with me? Work out on my machine?"

"Anytime. We'll set regular hours."

She grinned, her eyes lighting with laughter. "Wear spandex racing pants, a helmet, and ride bicycles with me?"

He paused, considering the tiny, girdlelike rig, which would cover part of his thighs and let everyone know everything about his body. She was teasing him now, but making Lilah happy was worth the tormenting he would take from the locals. "Uh-huh."

"You really mean it, Clint," she murmured finally, thoughtfully. "You won't laugh at me and you'll be open and sharing in our... relationship?"

"Sure do mean it. I'm serious and ready for being an intimacy-relating now-man." He wanted to gather her against him and cuddle her and tell her how sweet she was and how he'd craved her.

Lilah took a step nearer to him and smiled softly, placing her hands on his chest. She toyed with his top button and gently slid it open. Another followed until she pulled his shirt apart to look at his chest. "I've never really studied a man's body before, Clint—"

Her fingers played with his belt buckle and Clint sucked in his breath as she watched him with huge, dark eyes, filled with questions that caused him to swallow. In another minute, he'd be kissing her, plucking her off her feet and carrying her into the bedroom....

"What's between us is new," he murmured unsteadily. "I just hope I don't make any mistakes."

She grinned quickly, her expression filled with delight. "Is that what you were thinking just then? Really, Clint? I'm just as terrified."

"Good," he said. Honor made him add, "I want you badly."

Her fingers gently gripped the hair on his chest. "Clint? You don't think I'm too old to want sensuality? To want what I've missed? Or rather, just tasted years ago?" she asked, concerned.

"You have a right to know who you are," he answered honestly. "To be true to what lies within you. To explore what you need to be happy."

"And to explode?" she probed, watching him closely.

Clint swallowed and glanced down at the deep crevice between her soft, gently raised breasts.

"You're blushing, Clint," Lilah said gently, placing her hands along his cheeks. "You'd better take down that ad on the bulletin board. I think we should have dessert now—nice and rich and gooey to celebrate our new now-selves. We'll start on our pasta and exercise tomorrow. I've got ice cream and toppings and nuts for a banana split...."

Lilah knew Clint would hold "true to his word." He would try, though he had seemed horrified at her offer of a banana split with whipped cream. He had excused himself rather quickly from her apartment. He was out of breath when he ran up her stairs at six-thirty the next morning, but looked delicious, surly and off balance as he plopped his workout bag onto her floor. He stood in his cutoff jeans and bare chest and worn running shoes and panted, "Jogged two miles this morning...am out of shape...clothes in bag. I'll have to take a shower here to save time before church. What's first?"

He looked at Lilah's tight red-and-white-striped workout leotard and she stood very still. "Why do you want me?" she asked baldly, realizing that she knew what workout she wanted right then, right there.

The thought of Clint wanting to make love to her last night had kept her awake for hours. She had to know.

Clint inhaled, and continued to look at her in that hungry, breathtaking way. "Tell you later. Right now, I'm concentrating."

"Meditating? Oh, Clint, you meditate?" she asked, already impressed with his efforts.

He walked around her, studying her. "Mostly in the night. I've hummed to block out needs and thoughts. How did you get that thing on?" he asked with interest as his finger locked in the low-cut bodice and he tugged gently. "And what are you wearing that makes you so flat?"

"Sports bra."

"Mmm," he murmured, considering her shape. "Is this rig what everyone is talking about? Why Pete is suffering from eyestrain and why George is wanting to take his coffee break earlier in the morning?"

"They've been sweet. They encourage me to jog in place so I won't cool down too fast."

"Uh-huh. You bulge over the top of it." Clint's flat agreement questioned Pete's and George's motives.

"I know. But my exercise program will tighten me. What do you want to do, Clint? How about the bench press? Or I can bench press while you use the leg weights," she said, disturbed as Clint continued looming over her. He had the hungry look of a predator, which made her uneasy.

Clint Danner was wonderful on the bench press, lifting weights while his body lay flat on the bench. Lilah paused in her leg-weight-lifting exercises to admire his grace and beauty; she could not look away from his body—the flex of muscles and cords and dark skin. She absorbed and contemplated the response of her own body to his—the sudden warmth, the need....

He paused, looked at her and slowly lowered the weights. "Do it," he ordered very quietly. "Whatever you're thinking you want to do, do it."

Lilah gripped the leg weights for a lifeline, while Clint continued to watch her. "Our time is almost up. Would you like to shower while I fix bran and bananas? Then I'll shower...."

"No bananas," Clint said evenly, the image of the tray of bananas and protection skipping through his mind. "But we could help the environment . . . save water and shower together," he offered, still watching her.

"Naked?" she asked, jerking the weights too quickly and they zoomed high on the exercise device. She pulled them downward and realized her heart was leaping from joy, terror, excitement and very little from working out.

"Naked as jaybirds," Clint said very slowly.

"I...I don't know...." She hovered between her now-woman needs and the past—

"Fine. So much for that," Clint muttered and surged to his feet.

When he stepped out of the shower, Lilah was waiting for him.

She sat on the bed, uncomfortable, but ashamed that she had faltered when she did want that shower with Clint.

He emerged with a towel around his hips and brushing another over his head. His grim expression darkened when he saw her and he draped the towel around his shoulders.

They gleamed with tiny droplets of water. She could lick them off with the tip of her tongue—

Lilah kept her eyes above his shoulders. "I've never seen a man in the all-together," she stated, surrounded by his scents and shivering when his eyes lasered to hers. "A man might not want to look at me. I'm not a girl any longer, you know."

"I'd be honored if you'd let me," he murmured, tossing the towel from his shoulders onto a chair and padding over to her.

He stood in front of her, his towel slipping slightly from his hips and she glimpsed a pale line of flesh.

Lilah's entire body knotted and heated, yet she shivered. "Not today," she managed to say lightly, leaping off the bed and running into the bathroom.

She turned the water on cold, scrubbed herself furiously and shook with the knowledge that she had actually, almost-nearly reached out to touch Clint intimately.

To behold a wonder that she had never entirely seen.

He'd be dressed now, sheathed in the same old lifelong-friend image, and she'd missed her chance. Lilah jerked the belt of her robe tight and stepped from the bathroom.

Clint wasn't eating his breakfast in the kitchen. He was drinking his coffee and lying in her bed—still wearing the towel around his hips. It thinly covered his essentials from the waist down. "What's the plan?" she asked warily as she began to comb the tangles from her wet hair. "Aren't you going to dress right away?"

"Nope. I'm changing lanes into a now-man. I'm ready to relate to you. To tell you my deepest, most intimate thoughts. Come lie down here beside me."

"Under the sheet or over it?" she asked cautiously, now faced with everything she wanted. Would she take what she wanted as a now-woman, or would she falter again?

"Wherever you're comfortable. I want to tell you how I feel about this new intimacy thing and you." Clint placed aside his cup and turned on his side, making room for her in the narrow bed. He patted the space, the tiny sound echoed in her head like a rocket blast.

She eased onto the bed and looked at him.

She was in a bedroom—on a Sunday morning—with a man who was not her husband; she was grateful that she had removed Jeff's picture from her nightstand.

She had nothing on beneath her robe.

Clint wanted to talk about something that apparently was very important to him; she should listen and explore her thoughts along the way.

"How do you feel, Clint?" she asked carefully, then nervously added, "Do you think you'll be able to exercise in the mornings and work the entire day? Or maybe we should exercise in the evenings—"

"I loved Betty," he stated slowly. "I'll always love her and remember her and she'll stay in a part of my heart. But there's an empty part there, too, and it's needing filling."

"That's why you put your ad on the bulletin board," she offered quietly. "And decided to come out of the closet."

"That's it. Put your hand on my chest. There's a heart in here and it's seen its share of burdens and joy. Now it needs more than memories. What are you feeling, Lilah?"

"Scared," she said truthfully. "Really scared. If I make a mistake, I know I might not try again."

Clint smiled gently, looking very appealing with his morning beard and his hair damp and pushed back from his face. "That's how I feel. Scared. We'll make it. We're strong people, Lilah. Or at least I was until lately. Now I'm winded, and unless you kick me out, I'd like to try that relating business—sharing our thoughts. Come here," he ordered softly, watching her. "And tell me what you were thinking about when you looked at me on the workout bench."

She couldn't tell him that she'd wanted to straddle him and fit him between her thighs, squeezing him the way she pressed her thigh-tightener. Instead, she lay down very straight beside Clint. He placed his arm over her waist, his hand caressing her stomach. "Touch me," she told him shakily, refusing to give way to her fears. "Touch me, Clint."

His hand stopped and pressed flat against her. "I don't know if I'm up to all of this relating business," he murmured unsteadily as his hand framed her face, turning her lips slowly toward his. "But this is what I want now."

His kiss was beautiful, light and searching, cherishing her lips until she answered in hungry little hunting kisses of her own. She gripped his damp, corded shoulders and gave herself to the wonder and the beauty and sweet heat of his mouth.

Trembling with the needs rising within her, Lilah tried to lie very still.

The now-woman within her rebelled. "I can't have this," she whispered against Clint's warm, seeking lips.

He kissed her jawline and nibbled her ear. "Mmm?"

Lilah pushed at him, her hands flush on his chest. She paused in her thoughts to enjoy the crisp texture of the hair beneath her fingertips and the scent of a freshly showered man—her familiar friend Clint—swirling around her. "It's the 'what's first on the list problem,' Clint. I mean...who does what first. I mean...I asked you to touch me, but you decided to kiss, instead. So you're—as the conventional, old-fashioned male— you're setting the pace. You're leaving me little option but to follow your lead."

"It's a thing you work up to, Lilah," Clint stated cautiously.

"Oh, sure. When *you* set the pace.... When *you* decide that the time is right—"

She stopped talking as Clint's warm hand slid slowly lower on her body, parting the robe. His fingers curved gently over her femininity, caressing her.

Lilah's eyes widened as his touch eased within her and she shook, staring up at him helplessly as waves of heat dashed against her, within her, and her body tightened into a warm knot. She held very still, wrapped in her tangled emotions, the past and the present, the girl and the woman, as Clint's gaze met hers.

Their eyes locked with messages that she feared, yet wanted.

The tightening drew low within her, her eyes and her hands locking to Clint as he took her higher, then one touch caught her, riveted her in a high, tight cry that poured though the shadowy room and her body, dropping in tiny gleaming warm liquidy bits around her. "Clint," she whispered shakily, afraid to release her grip on his shoulders.

"Clint," she whispered again, searching his rugged face, the familiar, endearing, yet new planes and shadows...the slightly swollen line of lips she had once considered hard and grim. His name was enough. Her friend, the strength that had been in her life for so long, now kept her safe in the warm shredding of the past and the future, and the beginning of—the beginning of Clint, a man with whom she wanted to share the deepest part of her being.

"Yes. Clint," he said firmly, slowly, and drew her to lie against him.

Her flushed face hid against his throat. The soft sweep of her lashes caused him almost to jump off the bed. "I cried out for the first time," she exclaimed unevenly. She had shocked herself, stunned at her grasping, hot need, at the delight and wonder that had just passed.

"You surely did." Clint's chest lifted and he held his breath, slowly exhaled, then asked her quietly, "Are you sorry?"

She turned the newness, the intimate touch of him within her and shook her head. She'd wanted more.

"We can kiss now," she offered after a while, aware that she was nuzzling his throat.

"I don't think so," he returned in a deep, raspy voice, and his long body tensed and shuddered against hers. "But next time, you call the shots."

"That sounds fair," Lilah murmured and moved deeper in his arms, already drowsy. "You know, it's so strange, but I feel so relaxed, as if years of tension have just seeped out of me."

"If you want, I could return those videos to the agency in Potsburg," Clint offered lightly. "If you don't think you'll be wanting to date any of those men, that is," he added cautiously. "I'm going there Monday... ah... for tractor parts."

"Fine. I'd appreciate that, if you don't mind missing the sampling of exciting women...." She didn't want to share Clint or send him off to be excited by exotic now-women. Because she couldn't let him have his way entirely this time, she took his hand and drew it to her breast. He cupped her gently, his fingers spreading wide, his palm heating, comforting an ache that remained. His weight and strength soothed her as she drifted into sleep.

6

Lilah's tiny explosion in her apartment yesterday morning didn't help the tense, hungry need that rode Clint throughout his Potsburg shopping safari.

He wanted her to choose, to weigh the past and the future and determine what she wanted; yesterday he had almost—

Clint gritted his teeth for the hundredth time that day. He would wait and follow Lilah's now-woman plan.

He wanted her to be one hundred percent certain that she wanted him in every way. He wouldn't push her, but he wouldn't lose the small treasure she had given him. Lilah had been deeply shocked, her cry of pleasure quivering in the still, sweet shadows of her bedroom as she had burrowed her hot face against his throat.

She had turned to him for understanding and he wouldn't take advantage of that gentle moment by serving his need to become one with her.

To add to his physical discomfort, bananas never seemed more abundant in flat, dry, rural Oklahoma. While he shopped in Potsburg, bananas lurked at every street. Advertisements for banana cream pie, banana cake, banana splits and even banana-shaped bicycle seats in Potsburg's cycle shop leaped at him. A ladies'-dress-store window advertised a new color, "Hot Banana."

Every time he blinked, the image of various colorful foil packages on a tray seemed tattooed behind his eyelids. *I've never seen a man in the all-together...*

At four o'clock that afternoon, Clint backed his pickup to Lilah's patio. He'd made real advances in his "coming out of the closet" with Lilah and he didn't want to lose momentum. He'd spent a fortune and every penny was worth it, if Lilah lit up the way she did when they'd had dinner. She'd walked around him as if he were a vast, new interesting toy to be unwrapped with delight.

The shopkeeper who had sold him the silly flat little shoes to wear without socks that matched the pleated, loose pants, was grinning like a baboon with a banana—

Clint mentally erased that image.

After shopping, Clint had stopped at his ranch, hurried his watering chores and neatened his sparsely furnished house. He'd changed the sheets into the new black ones that no real man would hang up on the outside clothesline to dry. He'd purchased ylang-ylang-scented candles and thrust a variety of flower bouquets into fruit jars and parked a huge bouquet of red roses on his nightstand. He dusted and spread the new striped bedspread over his bed, tossed the new small pillows at the headboard and studied the effect. The stack of gentleman's magazines that he intended to read were hidden beneath the bed in the spare room.

Now, his pickup parked outside Lilah's apartment, he put off the moment of leaving the safety of his cab.

Clint frowned at poor old Mrs. Gentry as she puttered in her flower garden; he mentally repeated the fettuccine Alfredo recipe he'd learned and how to toss pasta against a wall to test its readiness. The wine was chilling; it had to breathe—whatever that meant—and the salad, apple and cheese makings were ready. Getting Lilah to view him as an interesting up-to-date male wasn't easy. He refused to try the unshaven look for men that had been suggested at the beauty parlor; he'd been uncomfortable as the slender young beauty operator had moved around him, trimming his hair. In his world before Lilah's now-woman stage, men went to barbershops with other men and *men-barbers* and they discussed crops and cattle.

Clint shivered. The beauty shop had been frightening. Women seemed to unpeel all layers of secrecy once they sat in the shampoo chair. He'd had his nails buffed just so he could stay longer, listening to the detailed, intimate chatter and see if he could pick up tips about how to treat Lilah as a now-woman.

His nails gleamed on the steering wheel and Clint scowled at them. He was thankful that the girl whose chest was in his face as she'd trimmed his hair was discreet. A professional, she'd understood his needs and had sent him home with a sackful of creams for rough elbows and hands, exotic-smelling after-shave that her husband loved and a variety of mysterious tubes and jars.

He'd had his first bird's-eye view of a woman having her legs waxed and had shuddered when the wax was removed. Women were tough— He reached to rub the tiny razor cuts on his legs....

The abrupt bump to his tires surprised Clint. Deep in thought, he'd allowed the pickup to roll, hitting a curb. He realized that any time he thought about getting close to Lilah, he seemed off in dreamland. Clint closed his eyes and fought the impulse to lay his forehead on his hands and brood.

He was a weary man being tried by too many tests; his pioneer forefathers had thought their lives were rough, but they'd never gone to beauty shops or shopping for pleated pants and no-heel shoes. They'd never asked clerks for videos on tightening pecs and rear ends. They'd never been squirted with a variety of spicy and tangy after-shaves and colognes, which took a good strong shower soap to remove. The goo that had stuck his hair in rocklike peaks took two doses of shampoo to remove.

Clint sighed tiredly. *Lilah was worth every minute of anything he had to do to make her see him as an interesting life partner, as a desirable man.*

He inhaled and decided that he couldn't prolong staying in the pickup's safety any longer. Clint eased from the seat and glanced at the two bicycles in his truck bed; the geared bicycles were ultralight and durable, measured to fit him and a clerk about Lilah's height.

He looked at the billiard parlor back door and knew that he'd finally made a total fool of himself.

Through the storage room's window, Lilah saw Clint's dusty pickup parked by her patio; she saw Clint, dressed in his typical faded western shirt and worn jeans. He fitted into the sunbaked prairie town, looking just as rangy, enduring and tough as his ancestors who had claimed the land. The broad brim of his hat shaded his expression, but she noted the tense set of his shoulders and the way he studied his polished, gleaming western boots.

His jaw moved as though he was muttering and he scowled at the two bicycles standing in the back of his pickup.

She frowned slightly, surprised that he'd arrived at an unusual time of day—he usually came over to spend the evening hours after going home and doing his chores.

Lilah flew out the door—driven by an excitement that just seeing him created. Her heart raced, images of Clint lying on her bed this morning, the scent of him around her as she awoke and found him gone—the heady knowledge that he had touched her as no other man had.

Suddenly shy, Lilah came to a stop just two feet in front of him.

He looked grim, as though he'd been through wars and had just returned for her—her hero. "It's been a long, hard day, Lilah," he said warily, a muscle in his jaw tensing. "Changing into a now-man isn't that easy."

"I know," she murmured sympathetically, wanting to cuddle him. "You weren't muttering to yourself a few minutes ago, were you?"

"What if I was?" he challenged, tipping his hat back on his head and spreading his legs in the typical western showdown pose.

"Do you think I'm past my prime? That I'm old and saggy?" she stunned herself by asking boldly. She held her breath and waited for him to answer, her hands balled into fists.

Clint's dark blue eyes looked straight into hers. "You're full and firmly packed. You've got curves that a man can find and lock on to," he said evenly, a dark flush rising in his cheeks. "You're a strong woman and a man needs that."

Encouraged by his answer, she pushed her luck. "Do you think I'm too old to want what I've missed, what I didn't know could happen between a man and a woman? That I want a relationship that's equal and exciting and romantic?"

Clint's gaze never wavered. "I'm proud of you. It takes a strong woman to find out what she wants and go after it."

He pleased her enormously, standing there in his western pose, legs locked at the knee. He glared down at her as though he'd fight anyone who disputed his statement. Then he said softly, "I like kisses in the daylight. Do you have one for me?"

Lilah's heart stopped; he'd given her a choice. What did she want?

She stood on tiptoe and placed her lips on his. Clint tasted familiar and dear and erotic. The combination had her locking her arms around his neck and holding him close. She tucked her face in the safe cove of his throat and shoulder and whispered, "Did I frighten you this morning when I...?"

He kissed her ear and nibbled her new heart-shaped stud earring. "Prettiest sound I ever heard."

Then Clint stepped her back from him, his hands stroking her shoulders. "We've got a lot of daylight left. If you want, we can ride these things out to my ranch and have dinner."

"Oh, Clint—you shouldn't have—oh, thank you, thank you, thank you," she exclaimed as he swung down the tailgate and began unloading the bicycles.

"Hop on," Clint said, holding the smaller one for her. "Here are the gears." He instructed her quietly, then glanced at Janey and Fred who had come to stand in the shade with Old Sam and Mrs. Gentry. "Bikes. We're going riding now."

"Fancy little dudes," Old Sam muttered, moving around the gleaming bicycles.

"July. Too hot for bike riding. You two aren't kids anymore," Fred warned.

"Shut up, Fred," Janey said pleasantly, beaming at Clint. "How wonderful of you, Clint. I wondered when this was going to finally happen. You go along now, Lilah, and have a good time. We'll mind the store."

Clint nodded and Lilah grinned at him as she circled a tree and tested the brakes, coming to a skidding stop in front of him. "I've got just the perfect outfit for bike riding," she said happily, remembering the sleek, neon pink-and-black, two-piece spandex. "But you can't ride in your jeans, Clint—"

"Why not? Jeans are good for everything, even church, if they're clean," Old Sam said in a stupefied tone.

Clint inhaled and nudged her shoulder, pushing her toward the stairs. He placed two plastic biking bottles in her hands. "I'll be fine," he said. "Go change. Fill these water bottles."

Lilah quickly changed, and as she stepped back out onto her porch, she looked down at Clint, who was talking with a small crowd excited about the bicycles. Their eyes met and locked. A new emotion caught her, held her as Clint watched her move down the stairs and she sensed his desire for her—for loving her and to please her. She sensed that she was coming to him almost like a bride—that he'd been waiting for her.

Her morning cry went echoing through the afternoon shadows and Lilah fought her blush. When she stood by him, he was the same old rugged-ornery Clint, the durable man and her friend. He was grimly determined to take her bicycle riding, defying the mind-set of Green Tomato's old-timers. She beamed up at him— her hero, her friend, her accomplice.

"Uh-huh," Clint said quietly as he glanced at her, as if "uh-huh" said volumes. She trusted him in this grand adventure, but when there was time, she'd want a full intimate conversation with him.

Clint fastened the water bottles on the bicycles and handed her gloves and a helmet. "Put these on."

He glanced at the crowd, gritted his teeth and tossed his western hat into the cab. Mrs. Gentry's eyes widened and Janey inhaled sharply as he unbuttoned his shirt, stripped it away to reveal a battered T-shirt. When he tossed his boots into the cab and began to unzip his jeans, Mrs. Gentry muttered prayers and Janey clasped her hands in front of her chest; she wore a delighted, excited expression of anticipation. Old Sam muttered ancient western curses about hell freezing over.

Clint's jeans gave way to spandex tights that went to midthigh, and he hurriedly jerked on loose shorts over them.

Lilah's heart quivered and warmed; she touched her hands to her head and with her eyes told him how magnificent he was. Clint's tight smile reached his eyes and she caught a glimpse of him as a boy.

Old Sam was aghast. "Clint Danner. You sure as shootin' shaved your legs."

"Italian bike racers do it," Clint replied in a dark, moody snarl.

"You ain't in Italy, boy," Old Sam noted.

"Don't you pick on him," Lilah ordered, standing in front of Clint. She faced the crowd who was studying Clint's gleaming, hairless legs.

"Ain't manly," Old Sam persisted, his leathery skin wrinkled into a mass of concern.

"He's all man," Lilah returned fiercely, and for some reason Janey's grin widened. Because Clint looked so warriorish, Lilah moved to his side and patted his hard rear for comfort; she wanted him to know her approval and she'd seen men offer the same comfort to their datemates. It seemed only fair.

Clint went very still and his eyes slowly lowered and locked to hers. "Now, that's intimate," he stated in a raspy whisper.

"Men do it," she challenged.

"Can't say I have in years," Clint retorted.

"It's equality. Are you shocked?" she asked teasingly.

"How would you feel if I did that to you?" he asked cautiously and Lilah found herself blushing and looking away.

Clint ignored Old Sam's colorful western exclamations with a determination that stopped the others. In minutes, he wore new athletic shoes. With a look, he dared Fred to utter one word and plopped a bicycling helmet on his head. He checked the fit and the chin strap of Lilah's and she wondered if their helmets would dent if she kissed him in the hard, fast way she wanted. Clint's dark blue eyes traced her face and brushed her lips; the air sizzled between them, tiny electric volts seemed to explode around their heads. "Let's go. We don't have all day," he said abruptly, getting on his bicycle as though they had ridden together all their lives.

People bumped into one another on Main Street. The sheriff followed them at a sedate distance as though protecting his town from possible celestial invaders.

Children zoomed down the streets and fell into a parade behind them.

The mayor's car ran into a fire hydrant, breaking it, and the children raced their bikes back to cool off in the waterfall. A series of wolf whistles with Clint's name attached echoed off the sunbaked brick buildings, and the undertaker came out of his funeral home to study the event as though waiting for possible customers.

Lilah wallowed in the thrill of the afternoon's event. She reveled in Clint's gesture to update the two of them. The first five miles passed easily; they experimented with gears and water bottles and rode side by side. They passed meadows and cows and sailed across the countryside and the sunset toward Clint's ranch.

Lilah felt light and young and carefree, the breeze sweeping over her body. She rode without touching the handlebars and stripped her T-shirt away, tucking it into a bag. "I hope you didn't shave your chest before I—" She clamped her lips closed.

Clint removed his shirt and she reveled in the sight of corded muscles, tanned skin lightly flecked with hair. She deliberately dropped behind to admire his rippling back and the set of his bottom on the bike's seat.

Then he turned to her, his dark blue eyes narrowing and he circled behind her. "Nice view," he said after a while and Lilah grinned. Clint Danner didn't make her feel middle-aged and out of shape.

"No man has ever cooked me dinner before," Lilah stated over the ylang-ylang-scented candlelight.

"What about breakfast?" Clint asked, thinking that if Lilah stayed in his reach, he'd take care of her needs. He inhaled as he moved to stand, carrying the dishes to the sink. Every inch of him was now rebelling against the ten-mile bicycle ride from town . . . and the confines of the spandex-girdle. Sitting at the table had allowed his muscles to react and now real pain was setting in.

Lilah seemed fine as she stood and stretched and carried the leftovers to the refrigerator. She yawned and moved to the couch, kicking off her running shoes along the way. She peeled away her socks and wiggled her red-hot tinted toes; Clint paused and decided she looked like a nymph in a fairy tale, all sleek and pink and curved. He wondered how to gently peel her out of that elastic rig as she said, "You know how breakfast is on a ranch. You're on your feet when the rooster crows, then there are chores and children and more chores."

She glanced at the sparse furnishings and Clint knew she understood his need to replace everything; he'd been drowning in memories.

He wanted to create new memories with Lilah.

Clint thought about ways he could keep Lilah's feet off the floor—if he could get her to spend the night. If she trusted him. If she wanted to make the choice, the commitment. He glanced at the clear moonlit night outside and remembered Alfred, his rooster. "Forgot to close the gate," he said. "Be right back."

Alfred didn't like being placed in a cage in the barn. He quieted when Clint hurriedly built a wall of hay bales to muffle the rooster's morning crows.

"You look cute in shorts, Clint," Lilah said when Clint returned to the house. Then, as he bent to sit by her on the couch, every muscle in his backside and thighs turned into immovable pain. He straightened slowly, looking down at Lilah, who had curled into a delectable picture of curves and big-eyed, hungry, mysterious woman.

There were men who called this look "ripe," but Clint didn't think of Lilah as a tomato to be plucked or reaped. He wanted to build a permanent foundation and didn't want to ruin the first building block by not rising to her challenge. "If you don't mind, I could use a bath. I got a little sweaty outside," he muttered, off stride and nettled because his calves had just begun to contract painfully. A few minutes of soaking might relieve the pain. "Or I can take you back to town now in my old pickup."

Lilah's wistful expression caught him. "Okay," she agreed quietly, her tone almost sad.

Clint froze. If she went home now... "Go home or wait awhile?" he pressed, his heart stopping while he waited for her answer.

"Go ahead and take your bath. I'll wait."

Minutes later, Clint drifted down into the hot water dosed with Epsom salts. He slowly flexed his legs and massaged them furiously. The pain lessened momentarily, then he stopped, hearing the knock on his bathroom door. "Clint, I want you to try this candle-bath thing. If you haven't tried it, that is. It's relaxing."

Nothing in Clint was relaxed; his muscles ached and his body needed, his mind couldn't stop thinking about Lilah's sweet morning cry and his hands longed for the shape of her breasts. "May as well go for broke," he muttered. He wanted her where he could see her, where he could be certain she wouldn't hop on her bicycle and ride back to her castle. "If you bring it in, I'll try it. We can talk. It will be part of an intimacy thing."

There was a long pause and another knock. Clint dropped a washcloth over his vitals and stirred up the soapy water into an opaque concealer. Lilah's gaze found him immediately, her eyes darkening as they lowered to his chest.

Clint stealthily adjusted the washcloth as she placed the lighted candle on the vanity. "I'll turn off the light for the full effect," she said, still looking at him. "You know, if you weren't taking a bath... I mean, if you were taking a shower instead, I'd..." Her words slid into the steam. "That water looks very hot, Clint," she noted.

If you weren't taking a bath... taking a shower instead, I'd...

Clint's body tensed; he forgot the onslaught of pain as he met Lilah's shy gaze. "Would you take one with me?" he asked slowly and prayed that he wasn't losing whatever was growing between them.

"I might," she whispered in a faint thread of sound that caused Clint's heart to race.

Without looking away, Clint said unevenly, "I'm draining the water."

Lilah's eyes widened, her lips parted and she quickly stepped outside the bathroom.

Clint groaned with pain and the knowledge that he'd gone too far, he'd frightened her. She'd be speeding back to town now, even though he'd offered to take her back in the extra pickup when she was ready. He gripped the sides of the tub, took a deep breath and gingerly rose to his feet.

He began to shower and shampoo quickly, fearing the idea of Lilah racing through the night—a drunken cowboy could—

"Clint?"

He flattened to one side as Lilah eased into the shower. "Is this going to work?" she asked, the water beating down on her head.

She was his heart, his love, his sweet Lilah....

"Yes," he heard himself say firmly in a tone like rusty barbed wire.

They stared at each other through the steam and the pounding water. The past seemed to wash away with each drop of water and an incredible sense of new tenderness quivered in the steam around them. Lilah's fingertip touched his chest; a thin thread of water ran from his body to hers, another link. Then Clint held his breath as her gaze slowly lowered. "Oh, my," she whispered above the sound of the running water.

Then the curtain parted and she stepped out of the shower. Clint turned off the water and tried to lift his leg over the side of the tub. Wrapped in pain, he stood there and mentally cursed his age versus his wants. He strained to lift his foot and groaned.

"Clint?" Lilah asked hesitantly after a few moments.

He closed his eyes and decided to admit his failure to her. "Lilah, I'm stuck."

"Stuck?" She tugged away the curtain and handed him a towel, which he wrapped around his hips. He noted that she was wearing a clean T-shirt of his. She looked cute and warm and sexy. And he couldn't move. "Clint, you look like you're in agony. What's wrong?"

"I'm out of shape," he admitted gloomily and knew in his deepest awareness that Lilah would cull him out right then.

Lilah concentrated on helping him gently out of the tub and onto the new sheets on his bed. Once he got the hang of letting her "oh" and sympathize... "Being an out-of-shape old cowpoke isn't that bad," Clint heard himself saying as Lilah looked at him from head to toe as though examining a new hobby and wondering where to start.

"I want you, Clint," she whispered, her expression worried.

Agony ripped through him when his muscles tensed. An aeon zipped by while he inventoried his wills and his can'ts. "Take me," he offered. He mentally applied one of Old Sam's ancient western curses to the bicycle.

"I want to dominate, take you where you lie, in the most hurried, almost primitive way."

"Do it," he said raspily, aching for her.

Lilah looked like a bride, he thought—his bride, on her wedding night. They'd have a lifetime of loving if he could just manage not to frighten her too badly. "How do I start?" she asked, still standing beside the bed. "I mean...I've never made a first move."

"You'll figure it out," he encouraged her.

"Are you aroused? I mean, are you in the same mode as I am?"

Clint gripped the satin sheets and closed his eyes. He'd wanted to reach for her, to draw her into his arms to soothe her. "Just how primitive are you feeling?" he asked.

She inhaled and shivered. "Very. I could hurt you, Clint.... Like I've waited a long, long time, and I'll explode if we touch."

Clint realized small droplets of sweat had formed on his upper lip. "I'm pretty close to that myself," he whispered.

Lilah sat gently on the bed and Clint took her hand, caressing her palm; he was glad that the muscles above his waist still worked. "Take your time, Lilah," he said. "We've got all the time we need."

Her fingertip strolled over the black satin. "Just how many women have been sizzled and mashed upon this bed, Clint Danner?"

"Not a one," he answered honestly. "I've been saving myself and my bed for you for years."

Her gaze lingered on his towel. "I want to place protection on you, Clint," she stated firmly.

"Fine. Do it." Clint prayed he wouldn't lose control and that parts of his body still obeyed his mind.

"Now? Or closer to . . . ?"

"We could kiss first. Try some intimacy talk."

She curled down against him fitting sweetly against his side as though she belonged there. "So you're not intimidated if a woman makes the first move?"

Lilah's toes caressed his legs and she wrapped her arm around him. "Not every yahoo would shave his legs to wear those pants," she said in an approving tone.

Clint fitted her perfectly, Lilah thought as she rested on him, their bodies locked as one. She tested the strength of her intimate muscles, the ones she'd been exercising while pushing her grocery cart and at other times, as well. Clint started, his body thrusting upward, deeper within her, and startled, she jerked away. "What was that?" he asked roughly.

"Muscle tone," she answered, shaken by his reaction. "Do you like it?"

"Yes," he whispered unevenly as she eased down upon him and moved experimentally.

She savored his patience when she was attempting her new skill, and she loved his kisses as he lay beneath her.

Clint tasted like forever—sweet, gentle Clint . . . her trusted friend and now, her lover.

She eased her hips down on Clint and his dark blue eyes closed as if he was concentrating very hard on her. He felt so solid beneath her, so wonderful and strong within her. His hand touched her breasts, his lips treasured her, and Lilah cried out with the beauty of making love with Clint.

She wanted to dive into him, wrap herself in his scents, his feel and revel in the racing pounding of their bodies. She gloried in his strength withstanding her might and tossed away the last shreds of keeping Clint safe—he was on his own. She caught him fast, her intimate muscles gripping him tightly as the pulsing heat and excitement sent her crashing again and again upon him.

When he suckled her breast, flicking her with his tongue and gently nibbling her sensitized flesh, her body betrayed her shredded control. Clint reached between them to touch her, she ignited and flew and burned, slowly drifting down to rest upon his safe, warm chest. She luxuriated in the way his hands had locked to her bottom, anchoring her to him and caressing her. She refused to let him leave her, her body tightening instinctively to keep him within her. "No, you're not going anywhere," she managed to whisper, shaken by what had passed and wanting fiercely for it to happen again—though her bones resisted her need to fly at the moment.

She draped herself comfortably on top of him, meshing her chest and stomach and thighs just as close to his rougher textured ones as possible. She wanted them glued together until she could manage to rummage enough energy to begin again and this time, she'd take Clint with her to the exploding stars.

Clint groaned and nuzzled and sighed his way free, gently escaping her feeble grasp.

Feeling like a limp, boneless, drowsy, damp, heated grin, she couldn't let him go, not even as he arranged her beside him beneath the sheet. She tangled him with her arms and legs and grumbled about her foiled foreplay plans, which earned her a rich chuckle.

Lilah awoke later, surrounded by the strength and the scent and the comfort of Clint. She tensed immediately, realizing that they lay "naked as jaybirds" and tangled in his black satin sheets.

She lay quietly, watching the moon-shadows play in the room, and realized that she needed him in the most intimate way.

Clint. Her friend. Her husband's friend... Her lover... Had he been happy with her?

Had she frightened him? Would he regret her fumbled attempt to sheath him in protection?

Would he laugh at her and go on his culling ways?

They hadn't talked after she'd taken him. *Had she acted selfishly, pleasing herself and leaving him?* Good Lord, she had actually ridden him like some wild—

"Deep thoughts for the middle of the night, Lilah," Clint murmured, turning on his side and nuzzling her hair.

"Clint, I was brought up to be a lady.... Behaving like some wild woman," she muttered, fearing he would laugh at her unruled first attempt, so quickly over. Clint, for his part, was very controlled.

Maybe she wasn't adequate.

Maybe she didn't excite him.

Terror ran through Lilah. "I'm not good at this," she stated flatly.

"What?"

"Good Lord, Clint, you don't even know what! I just made love for my very first time with my best friend— yes, that's what you are, Clint. I've ruined our friendship and maybe ruined you for women in general. I've slaked my...needs upon you and had my way with you and you probably obliged because you're a caring person, merely helping me to— Oh, Clint, I've ruined everything!" she wailed, pulling the sheet over her head. "Our friendship...years gone because of my selfishness, my insatiable need to be a now-woman."

Clint ducked his head under the sheet. "You're not going to run off now in that snit before I have my chance to talk, are you? Because parts of me aren't exactly delighted with your first adventure."

Lilah turned to him under the folds of the sheet. In the darkness, he looked more familiar. At least he didn't look as stressed as when she'd pinned him beneath her. "See? I knew I disappointed you."

"You have pleased me more than I ever dreamed about," Clint said firmly.

"I wanted to play a bit, Clint," she protested and wiped away a tear that had been seeping from her lids. "You know...games...adventures...make myself a sensual woman...just a light touch here and there and then at the end we'd sort of...burst together.... My pacing is wrong—I *don't* have pacing. I probably don't have sensuality. It's gone. . . . I probably never had any, anyway. I've missed my chance for foreplay—just pushed it aside—and the afterplay—"

She realized she had wailed the last word forlornly. Her tone didn't change as she admitted, "Clint, I still haven't seen a man in the all-together without steam and water, and you had to finish . . . doing what I started."

So much for following easy 1-2-3 directions and practicing; she couldn't even sheath him in protection. She would have had to touch him—

"We'll work through this," Clint murmured, pulling her rigid body against his. "Are you hurting?"

Lilah closed her eyes and inventoried her most intimate depths; she decided that she felt lush and happy and— "No. Am I supposed to be?"

She ignored his rich chuckle and gave herself to the familiar caress of his hand. Then she fastened her fingers onto the safety of his shoulders and demanded, "Am I a failure, Clint? Shouldn't I have known how to pace and—"

"I thought you did just fine. I was thinking maybe you might want to try again."

She shook her head fiercely; she didn't want Clint to act as her martyr. "No. I forgot myself and ruined everything."

He stroked her hair with one hand that slid down to soothe her tense shoulders. He gently slipped her body against his and inhaled slowly, "It's your choice. But the first time was sweet as honey, rich as dew on a morning rose."

"I'm not in the mood for sweet talk, Clint. This is a pretty frightening experience for me. I've shocked myself. I can't promise anything if I try again," she told him resolutely as Clint lifted her slightly and began nibbling on her breasts. He eased her over him and they lay like that, looking at each other solemnly.

"You're very hard," she noted after a full minute had passed. "Is this a nightly thing?"

"Constant, every-night-and-day thing since you started being a now-woman. You're pretty exciting," he returned with a small, tender smile.

"Like warmed-over mush," she muttered. "For all my talk, I'll probably never get the hang of my sensuality."

"Like a red-hot chili pepper," he said in a raw tone.

"You're sweet, yourself," she returned, encouraged by his remark. She eyed him beneath her, his tousled, endearing, rumpled look and the night's stubble crossing his jaw. "This means something to me, Clint. I want you to know that."

"Me, too. Means we care for each other. We trust each other. Means we have a relationship, doesn't it?"

"So we've crossed from friendship into something else?" she asked, her throat tight. Dealing with what-happens-first, whose responsibility what is, being a now-woman and plain old Lilah wasn't that easy, especially if she tossed in how much she wanted to become a part of him again.

Was it wrong to want him so much, so intimately, to want him to feel as she did at the peak of her explosion? To hold him as he held her later?

"I didn't think I'd ever do this again," she whispered to her friend-lover, her intimate-counterpart. "I've failed. It's just like everything in life went on and I stopped somewhere just after point A. Oh, Clint, I thought I was past so much . . . past the fear and excitement— Oh, Clint, I'm not comfortable at all with this. I feel like I'm nineteen again on my wedding night. Only this time, I'm the impatient one."

"Are you all talk or can you kiss a bit in between?" Clint asked gently, kissing the tip of her nose.

"Can we kiss and make love at the same time?" she asked, curious now.

"Come here and we'll try it," Clint murmured as he tugged her head down to his.

"Aren't I too heavy, lying on top of you like this?" she asked breathlessly after the first, long, hungry kiss.

"You feel like a feather, all soft and cuddly," he whispered, easing her hand down to him.

She drew away, unused to the familiarity. "Clint, I really don't know that I can do any better the second time," she whispered shakily.

He stroked her hair and kissed her neck and a great shudder swept through his body. "I'd really appreciate a second effort," he whispered hoarsely.

"When's the foreplay and afterplay? We can't just—" She cried out as he entered her, his hips lifting her slightly.

Dawn arrived sometime before her first explosion and day arrived fully as she slid down by Clint's side and snuggled close to him—Clint, her intimate now-man... who had whispered endearments and encouragement while they made love.... While she made raging love to him....

7

—➤◆◄—

Lilah leaped out of bed, grabbed her clothes and dressed as she ran to the front door and into the daylight. Clint called out her name and she stopped in midstride. Woozy and off balance, she jammed on her running shoes and didn't stop to tie the laces.

She'd skipped the suggested, enriching foreplay and afterplay, greedy for Clint Danner—her friend, her neighbor, a respected tractor franchiser—and had gone right for the bursting rockets and stars. Would he ever respect her again?

The July sun toasted the fields into golds and browns just as it always had. Cattle grazed in the pasture and the oil rigs on the horizon continued their infinite bobbing. Her life had zoomed off on an uncertain angle and yet the Oklahoma prairie went on as it had since pioneer times. She blinked, blinded by the morning sun.

The warming, gentle morning air settled like silk on her skin. She stood very still, aware that her body had changed. Right now her skin felt too tight and intimate muscles ached.

Lilah closed her eyes, remembering the lock and fit of their bodies, remembering glancing at Clint's bedside clock. The time was six o'clock. No one in Green Tomato's farming country slept in on a hot day; they were halfway through their chores by now.

At forty-three, she'd just made love in the daytime. She'd spent the night and an hour since dawn in Clint Danner's bed.

What should she say to him? What was the morning-after etiquette? Should she cook him breakfast? She remembered movies where the couple lay smoking in bed after lovemaking. But neither Clint nor she smoked. Then in other movies, the lovemakers seemed to have a cold businesslike mood afterward. She could never, never feel that detached, as if she were just taking care of a body necessity and her emotions weren't involved.

Should she tell him she loved him?

She'd planned to have him and now that she had, what were the rules?

Clint called her name again and she heard furniture crash in the house. She wanted to run back to the safety of his arms, his deep soothing drawl. She wanted her old friend, Clint, and the safety of the past.

She wanted the future. She wanted to meet Clint Danner as a now-woman, a woman who knew who she was and what she wanted.

She bent to tie her laces and thought how knotted together their lives were, how complicated everything was now—the morning after her first now-woman experience.

Not that the qualifications for being a now-woman ran to loving a man.

Lilah hopped onto her bike and began pedaling very fast as scenes of Clint making love with her came zipping to her.

She hadn't excited him into a full steam.

But she would. He fit her fine. She just hadn't expected to get hit with love and rockets and shocking needs.

She wanted to race back to Clint and test his skills at relational-intimate talk.

She needed to watch more soap operas and weigh if a person her age could really feel this shattering, primitive love.

Her first love had been sweet and tender and conventional; she didn't feel that way about relating to Clint.

Her intimate muscles contracted suddenly, surprising her and she almost ran into the ditch.

A relationship with Clint Danner...a sexual heat and storms and exploding stars... Her body jerked into one tight knot and she cried out with surprise.

If she had Clint within her grasp, she decided angrily, *she'd make him pay for upsetting her. She'd have her revenge by squeezing him so tight with her new thigh-tightened muscles that he'd beg for mercy.*

Lilah passed Spud Jones's battered cattle truck and he honked. Billy Jo and Susie Ann Willis honked as she sped past their pickup loaded with hay. Orly Riggins rang the bell perched on his big tractor and Maizie Samms waved from her front porch.

Lilah's face flamed in the heat and embarrassment. The townsfolk all knew she was coming home from a night spent at Clint's. ''Just out for an early-morning ride,'' she called to Lisa Farris, who stood in her curlers and robe.

Clint eased into his old pickup's cab, his leg muscles taut and screaming with pain. At four o'clock in the afternoon, he'd just managed to shower and remove the strong liniment smell from his body. Continuing to work his muscles throughout the day only reminded him of Lilah's fitness and his inability this morning to rise and follow her. He was determined to recoup his losses in the pursuit of Lilah McCord. Sober determination kept him stretching and soaking and massaging throughout the day and he was now exhausted, but able to move. His body throbbed with a painful reminder that his night of love with Lilah McCord wasn't totally complete. A phone call to his employee, Marvin, had excused him from working during the day.

Clint inhaled as he placed his boots on the clutch and the brake of the old pickup and shook his head.

He hadn't had a chance to treat her like a bride, to sprinkle rose petals over her or ask how she felt. He'd wanted to whisper how she'd filled his heart with her beautiful gift and how— She'd hurried from his bedroom and was riding her bicycle back to town before he could limp to the front door.

Fear and horror leaped in her expression as she had paused and looked back at him. She'd looked like a sweet, terrified fawn running from a wildfire. That wasn't the look he wanted Lilah to wear after spending the night cuddled close to him. The pickup squalled to life and Clint grimly drove to town, wondering what he would say to Lilah.

She'd been stunned—awakening to him stretched out beside her.

The guilt on her expression could be easily read.

He scowled at a bull sniffing the wind and cow d'amour. If Clint could have moved this morning, he would have made love to Lilah again—offered her the reassurance and tenderness she deserved.

He'd never had a woman run from him in his life.

Everyone had seen them ride out of town the evening before, and only Lilah McCord rode back the next morning.

Clint screeched the gears on the old truck. He'd let her down at a delicate moment in their relationship. He should have run after her.

When Clint pulled into town, Lilah, dressed in her bicycle-riding spandex and her helmet, zipped by a side alley. Edward Jamison, lurking on the sidewalk and dressed in bicycling gear, zoomed toward Lilah, chatting with her as they rode along. After a moment, Lilah lowered her head in racing form and left Jamison as though he were standing still. He pedaled rapidly, then quickly sagged and stepped on the side of the road, a defeated challenger.

Clint smirked; Lilah was a strong woman and Jamison couldn't keep up. His smirk died when he recognized the direction Lilah's bicycle was taking.

Lilah McCord was riding out of town, toward his ranch.

Clint revved the pickup, placed it into reverse and drove onto a side road concealed from Lilah by trees. He jammed the gears, crossed the creek, the Johnsons' meadow and the old rocky field to the back fence at his place. Because there wasn't a gate, Clint painfully maneuvered himself out of the pickup and clipped the barbed wire, driving through the pasture to his house.

He showered again because he'd worked up a sweat in his racing, rummaged through the refrigerator to prepare a Greek salad filled with greens, olives and mushrooms and walked outside to find Alfred the rooster.

Alfred didn't want finding. But in fifteen minutes, he was tucked in his muffled cage; Clint quickly showered again and changed clothes. He brushed his hair, studied the new man dressed in a loose shirt and slacks, then spotted his mussed bed in the mirror.

He hadn't wanted to change the sheets with Lilah's scent— In fact, in his pain throughout the day, he'd wrapped himself in the encouragement they offered... Lilah McCord as his love. Clint ripped away the black satin sheets and replaced them with clean creamy-colored new ones just as Lilah's bike slid into his ranch yard.

She looked back at the road and Clint held his breath, realizing that if she decided to ride back to town— She lifted the helmet free and shook her hair, looking at the house.

Lilah McCord was one glorious piece of curved, succulent, tender-strong woman. Pride swelled and blossomed within him like a big Texas yellow rose; he thought he smelled jasmine, orange blossoms and ylang-ylang; meadowlarks seemed to sing and twitter around his head and his whole body felt like one big goofy smile—and Lord, how he loved her....

John, Clint's son, called at that moment. "Dad, what's this I hear about you putting the moves on Lilah McCord? Stacy said you shaved your legs and you and Lilah rode out of town last night on bicycles. Today, she's humming and all decked out in a Sunday dress and it's a Tuesday. Marvin said you didn't show up for work today and that this morning Lilah rode back into town by herself. What's happening?"

Lilah's hot-pink striped bicycle suit moved past Clint's window and he said, "I'm getting married to Lilah McCord. Either that or we're going to be significant others. It's a new lifetime thing. Don't call back."

"Dad," John protested when Clint replaced the receiver.

"Clint, did last night and this morning really happen?" Lilah asked worriedly when he opened the door. Her eyes widened as she looked down his cream-colored shirt to his tan slacks. "Clint, that's a gorgeous out-fit," she exclaimed. "Take it off."

"You first," he invited unevenly as Lilah's expression changed to sheer horror.

"I didn't mean to say that. You're not just my learning toy," she whispered, her expression anxious. "All this means something, but I haven't figured out just what. I'm too busy trying to understand how I could...how I could just...take you. You didn't have a chance, Clint. You were all but staked out and helpless—at my disposal."

She glanced at the bedroom and flushed.

"Wild woman," Clint teased softly and drew her into his arms.

Lilah latched her arms around his waist and huddled to him. "I've shocked myself down to my toenails. I want to apologize for whatever damage I've done to you. You poor, poor man. Do you think we could forget what happened last night? I mean the...ah..."

"Lovemaking?" Clint questioned softly, fear trembling inside him. If she regretted last night, his heart would shatter. Clint had never felt so fragile.

"I couldn't stay home, not when I knew you were injured, aching and in such pitiful shape when I left this morning. You weren't even able to work today...all because of me...because of my— Oh, Clint...I zapped you, I know I did. Twice. I didn't even give you the thoughtful foreplay and afterplay. Oh, Clint, everyone saw me ride back to town this morning—"

He drew her tighter against him; he'd protect her with his last breath. "Did anyone say anything?"

Lilah gripped his new shirt by the lapels and asked him fiercely, "How do you feel, Clint?"

How did he feel? Like kissing her... like asking her to share his life, his home, his future. Like telling her he loved her.... And everything wrapped in one huge, frightening terror that she would walk away from him.

"I want details, Clint," Lilah pressed, her expression deeply concerned. Then, without waiting, she tossed questions at him. "Do you realize how old I am? I mean, I'm not a girl any longer. I mean, I'm all excited about everything, quivery inside and flushed and anxious to hold you and know that it was all true. Then there's more and it...it's all so frightening, Clint," she whispered, suddenly drained. "I never felt so charged, so ready to—"

She leaned tiredly against him. "I'm wrinkling your new shirt—and it's beautiful, by the way.... Oh, Clint, I feel foofy and greedy," she wailed softly.

While he dealt with that and the needs that holding Lilah in his arms could arouse, she continued, "I was just a girl when I married, then everything went so fast—the children, trying to get a financial start.... I haven't learned that much about myself."

"Exactly what does 'foofy' mean?" Clint asked cautiously. If "foofy" was a new now-woman word and he said the wrong thing... He mentally sorted through the new dictionary he was composing by watching soap operas; "foofy" did not appear.

Lilah burrowed against him and ignored his question. He stroked her back and prayed that he wouldn't fail her this time. "Oh, Clint. I've got that 'earthshaking, sweat-making, body-heating, sweet, breathless kissing and heart palpitating need. Do you think that's normal for a woman of my age? How do you feel about it? Don't you laugh, either, or you'll be barred from my billiard parlor."

Clint wanted to pick her up and carry her into his bedroom and show her his heart, his love. But his experience with Lilah was that she chose what was right for her when the time suited her. "Ah... how about a glass of lemonade to cool down?" he asked cautiously, deciding upon a middle-ground question.

She gripped his lapels tighter and glared up at him. "I notice you're not sharing in this intimate-relating business," she accused. "I thought you were going to talk more about your thoughts with me. If you've got any resentful feelings toward me about last night and my... immaturity, tell me now. I know that I ravaged you when you weren't capable...capable of defending yourself. Clint Danner, you've got the sort of old-fashioned male temperament that would resent a now-woman demonstrating her affections. I didn't go all over town boasting about staking you out on your black satin bed, you know. If you hurry, you could make up with Angie or Missy, or both, and not lose too much time over my little jaunt into learning about my uncertain sensuality."

"Am I being lectured?" he asked, nettled that Lilah wanted to remove herself from his loving. His *old-fashioned male temperament* grated.

"I've never stood nude in the moonlight," she told him suddenly, watching him carefully.

Clint realized his heart had stopped as he tried to hop on her thought-train. "As soon as the moon comes out tonight, we'll try that," he offered warily as Lilah's hands began skimming his shoulders as though sizing him for a fit.

Though his home was air-conditioned, Clint's body heated instantly as she stroked his chest. "I'm not an impulsive woman, Clint. You know that. I've worked to make my business a success and hope that my children consider me a good mother and a good home-maker. You know that I received first prize for my watermelon preserves and zucchini bread and prune jam. I was a home-room mother and a leader in the girls' clubs. I am always active in helping with the county fair. But right now, on this edge with you, there are things I'd like to do that would—"

Clint's hands locked on to Lilah's soft spandex-covered bottom. "Like what?" he asked when he could speak.

"I've never once undressed a man. Unzipped and unbuttoned a man's clothes. Just how are your muscles now? Hurting?"

"I'm fine," he lied, his body knotting instantly with the need to carry Lilah to his bed.

"Is that why your body is like a board? Why you're so tense?" she asked, placing her palms on either side of his face and looking up at him with concern.

"I've got things on my mind," he murmured with honesty as Lilah's breasts pressed into him gently. He locked his hands on her hips, his fingers splayed over the spandex.

"Like what?" she asked curiously. "Tractor parts... stock racks... cattle prices... drought?

"Like peeling this rig off you and getting you back in my bed. I want to show you what I'm feeling, because the words sure aren't coming. I failed you this morning, Lilah."

Her eyebrows shot up. "Failed? I thought you were magnificent. You mean, we... ah... we can get even better?" she asked, excitement flushing her face. "I didn't notice you... ah... being extremely happy with the event."

He cleared his throat. "When a man sets out to seduce a woman, he ought to perform a bit better on the morning after. He should be able to still the woman's fears and pick her up and hold her close and tell her what's in his heart—"

Lilah's fingertips pressed into his shoulder. "Seduce? *You* wanted to seduce *me?*" she said in an amazed tone. "Why?"

Then, while he was thinking how to tell her that he wanted a long-term relationship, Lilah looked at him with widening eyes. She withdrew a bit and gazed down at his new clothes and cautiously sniffed the new after-shave he'd just used. "The satin sheets? The flowers? Throwing pasta at the wall? That was supposed to seduce me? Clint, you've made me so happy!" she exclaimed. "Imagine that... you cared enough to seduce me," she said wonderingly. "You are truly a nice man. You didn't do it out of pity, did you, Clint?" she added immediately, shifting emotional gears and clutching his shirt.

She frowned up at him while he was searching for the right words. "Oh, Clint. You didn't do it because you've run out of dating selections, did you?"

"My satin sheets are new, just for you. A man doesn't sleep on satin sheets hereabouts. I wanted you," he stated seriously. "I wanted you tight and hot against me. I wanted you to look at me as a man. Like a woman looks at a man that she's... that she's wanting." He couldn't say loving; he'd frighten her. "I even watch soap operas to find out how men treat now-women," he admitted in a defiant tone.

She chewed on that silently. "You went to all this work, just to seduce me?"

He knew he'd failed miserably and the reminder nettled. "Now, Lilah, don't go off and... It was my mistake not to follow you and alleviate your fears. That doesn't mean I'll fail the next time."

He inhaled grimly. "I had a problem this morning—pain. But I'll get in shape, Lilah. What's between us isn't just a temporary thing, you know. If I could have moved, you wouldn't have been able to jump out of bed and run off like that."

Her fingers tightened in the material of his shirt and she tugged him closer. "What's this mean, Clint? What's happening? Why on earth would you want to seduce me?"

"Because you make me hot," he answered truthfully. He intended to say more...things about lifetime loving and sharing, but stopped when Lilah beamed up at him.

"I do? *I* make you hot?" she asked, amazed. Then she frowned. "You seemed so...controlled last night."

"If I could latch on to you right now, I'd do it," he said evenly. "And if I could, I'd keep you in bed for a solid week. That's how controlled I am."

"Is that a normal thing to do, Clint?" she asked worriedly. "I mean at our ages?"

"How do I know?" he asked, frustrated with himself and the way he hadn't told her about his heart needing her.

"The national average is two or three times a week, isn't it? Clint, we used up the total national average in one night!" she mourned softly. "And it seemed to go so fast."

He didn't tell her that one of them hadn't used the national average once. "It isn't a thing you budget," he offered carefully.

"You should know," she affirmed thoughtfully, reminding him that he'd nipped a few blossoms in past years. "But I want to tell you that I am highly flattered that you wanted to seduce me. I think I'll go home now and ponder all this. But I also have to be honest with you, Clint. Sometimes I look at you and I just feel like I could kiss the daylights out of you. One time I even thought about kissing you all over, in the all-together," she admitted unevenly. "I know that I'm too old for these feelings, but I have them just the same. I suppose now I've really frightened you, huh?"

"Well, I don't know," Clint said, sliding his hand over her breast and capturing her heartbeat in his palm. "Just how would you kiss me when you did all this kissing? Would you leave me enough air to breathe?"

She considered the matter and placed her hand over his, pressing it tighter against her. "There would be sucking, of course, and nibbling, and I think I've gotten the hang of kissing and breathing at the same time. But kissing and breathing and making love with you— I don't know. Oh, Clint. I am truly aghast at this volcano of emotions within me. Truly. I think I could nip you a bit if I really let go. Isn't that awful?"

Clint had a problem with his own volcano. He would not push Lilah with his declaration of heart-filling love, of wanting her forever; he knew her well, and when Lilah chose, she chose very carefully.

He wanted to be her choice, her love. He realized that more was at stake than physical loving, though his body protested a certain lack right now.

"Clint, if I released what I am feeling now, I would frighten you. I've never been a primitive person, but there's just something about you touching me that sets me off. It scares me because I never thought I would feel like that."

He glowed from his innards to his out-ards. In another minute, he'd be floating.

"I have to be honest with you, Clint. You have truly stirred me and I'm not certain how to deal with this. I never expected the need to rip off your clothes, or explore you, or hold you— It's a fierce and mighty need."

His need for her was just as fiery, but he wasn't taking chances with Lilah's heart.

Lilah's honey brown gaze slid slowly downward to the vicinity of his pleats, and she murmured something about "nubbin." "I'd better go now."

Clint followed her out to the porch, leaning against a post for support. He jammed his shaking hands into the pockets of his pants because he didn't have a good old-fashioned western belt to grip. Lilah got on her bike and stood looking at him, her uncertainty written on her expression.

"See you," she said lightly.

Clint's stomach knotted. Just *See you.* "Running away, Lilah?"

She frowned. "Don't you start with me, Clint Danner. I came to check on you out of the goodness of my heart."

"These fancy duds should rip easy if you had a mind to try it," he offered and fought the frustration rising within him.

The afternoon sunlight glinted off her helmet as she stared at him. "How many women have ripped off your clothes?"

"Not a one and if you want the truth, there haven't been that many. Rumors get bigger with time." Sunlight danced through the shadows of the old trees shading Clint's yard and the cattle lowed in the field, just as they had for all time. Yet, with Lilah working her way through the events that had passed between them, time seemed to skid to a stop.

She looked at the post where Alfred liked to crow and Clint almost felt guilty about caging him. "How many women have you seduced?"

"I haven't been able to do any real seducing yet. Want to stay and let me practice?"

She flushed, pushed her bike and lowered her head and body into racing position, heading toward Green Tomato and safety.

"Mother?" Olympia's voice asked from the message recorder when Lilah got home. "Why are you racing all over the countryside at odd hours of the day and evening?"

"Mother?" Rosemary's voice asked in the following message. "Why is Clint Danner's pickup parked by your back door? Is he sick and did you take him to the hospital? Mom? Did he have to lie down in the back while you drove?"

There were several other jumbled messages from single men in town; Lilah had no idea why they would call her unless they wanted a special billiard tournament.

She called both of her daughters, reassuring them that she was safe and getting "buff" and that Clint…

that Clint was waiting for a part to repair his pickup and she had allowed him to park the truck at her house.

At eleven o'clock, after her shower and hours of staring at the moonlit wall, Lilah jerked on her new tropical-print silk robe. She jammed on her boots and went to Clint's pickup. She opened the cab and slid into the darkness scented of Clint.

A man like Clint Danner had probably never heard of ylang-ylang candles and yet he had provided them for her. Black satin sheets for a cowboy who used cotton. Fettuccini Alfredo and pasta sticking to the wall.

He'd been magnificent, tossing it at the wall with a flourish and grinning with pleasure when it stuck.

He watched soap operas to learn how to treat now-women.

And he'd set out to seduce her.... He'd thrilled her with that admission.

He'd worn spandex, the ultimate sacrifice for a man like Clint.

She lay down on the seat and hugged his clothing to her, smoothed his boots with her hand. She placed her feet outside the open window and arranged Clint's large clothing over her.

After a few restless, yet comforting moments of Clint's scent, Lilah opened her robe to discover that she hadn't a stitch on. She carefully arranged Clint's shirt over her bare breasts and his jeans over her legs, remembering how he had stripped right there in the daylight.

She smiled; Clint Danner had been magnificent, shaved legs, glare and all.

Few men would have his courage; a cowboy wearing spandex was asking for teasing.

Her smile widened. *And he'd wanted to seduce her.*

Her very first seduction. Not every man would go to the trouble that Clint had, right down to the satin sheets.

Lilah frowned. She wasn't a girl mooning over her first boyfriend. She was a widow with grown children and a grandson.

She'd loved and been loved by her husband long ago, and nothing that she remembered prepared her for how she felt about Clint Danner now.

The fierce need to hold him close, to have him cuddle her rose so swiftly, Lilah quickly folded Clint's clothes and started his pickup. "Prepare yourself, Clint Danner," she muttered as she drove through the night toward his ranch. She hoped he had recovered from his muscular pains because she didn't want to feel guilty tonight.

"Did you come to seduce me?" Clint asked as Lilah got out of the pickup and realized her bravado had soared to the moon.

She clutched her robe where it parted at her thighs and remembered she didn't have a stitch on beneath it. The curlers in her hair, designed to create spirals, acted like antennae. They picked up the tense vibrations running on the moonbeams between Clint and herself. "I brought back your pickup. People are asking questions about it. Why it's still sitting by my house.''

''Come here,'' he ordered huskily as she stopped at the steps to his house. In the shadows, Clint stood in his familiar western pose, his long legs sheathed in jeans. Excitement hovered in the moonlit distance between them.

''Give me one good reason why I should,'' she returned, knowing that she'd come to him for her own reasons.

''Tell me what you've got under that silk robe and I will. Do you always wear those things in your hair?''

''I want to try a spiral hairdo. How are you feeling? Muscles still hurting?'' she countered, and knew that she could get into the pickup and drive back to town if she wanted. Clint would let her go; he was a man who let people make up their minds without forcing them—

''I'm feeling like I need a moonlight bath,'' Clint drawled.

8

Clint Danner in his moonlit all-together, his lean hips sheathed in ordinary white undershorts, inspired Lilah. She kept her robe and boots on as they settled onto the air mattress and satin sheets that Clint had provided. "I don't understand any of this," she murmured.

In his western clothes, he was her old, familiar friend; he'd understand her uncertain emotions. But with his hard body—sheathed in that one, tiny strip of cloth—next to hers, her skin tightened and heated beneath the silk robe and she wasn't certain about him at all. Or herself. Right now, she was certain that every vibrant red silk flower on her robe was quivering.

"Just remember who I am," Clint noted wisely as he studied the stars overhead and drew her head to rest on his shoulder. He paused, moved slightly away and gently removed the foam curlers from her hair. He wrapped a spiral around his finger and studied it. "Who I could be to you and what's passing between us."

"I saw rockets exploding last night, Clint…and you didn't," she said sadly. "What went wrong?"

"You're combustible," he soothed, bending to give her a long, sweet kiss.

She eyed him. "And you're not?"

He shrugged a broad shoulder in the moonlight and nuzzled her curls. The tip of his tongue traced the whorls of her ear. "I thought I'd wait. No sense in hurrying."

"I do not wish to swoon alone," Lilah stated firmly, trembling as his lips surveyed her throat. "All this is not easy for me, you know. I have thoroughly shocked little sweet Lilah McCord who bakes cakes for church socials and sings in the choir...who has raised a family and been the president of the ladies' extension circle. I have new skills to learn before I feel up to par. This shifting-lanes-type thing isn't like baking a cake from a recipe, you know. I've got to feel out what is right for me."

"We could practice." Clint slid his hand inside her robe and she pushed it out again. When he touched her, her thought processes ran to having him lodged deeply within her; right now, she wanted to know more about their relationship.

She clung to his fingers, which had laced securely with hers. "Do you know how difficult it is to...to let go...of what I shared with Jeff and think of...this with you?"

"I truly do." His tone was firm, like a man taking his vows.

She squirmed on the air mattress and sniffed the fragrant earth scents and Clint's all-male ones. In another minute, she'd cry, uncertain emotions circling her. To divert herself, she asked, "Is this air mattress new? Why did you get a double size?"

Clint stirred and looked sheepish in the moonlight, his face all shadows and angles. "I had my dreams of some fool woman—namely, you—slaking our passions out here in the field. I thought you might romance me if I provided the mood. It's a seduction thing, Lilah. I had big plans to be the seduct-ee. But you got me so rattled showing up like that, that I forgot the wine and crystal glasses and the romantic tapes."

He inhaled sharply, then admitted in a disgusted tone, "I don't rattle easy, Lilah. But one look at you standing there in your red silk flowered robe and boots and these curlers is enough to rattle any man. You looked like a goddess in the moonlight." He glared at her. "You've got me drooling. I've been practicing my intimate talk—saying what's on my mind—and if you make fun of me, you'll never hear a bit of it again."

"Poor baby." Lilah held his hand and comforted him by stroking his chest. He was probably still shaken over her muscle-woman demonstration of zapping him twice. Clint needed more sensitivity from the woman zapping him.

She grieved for the loss of foreplay and afterplay, which she had tossed away in her fever to make love with him. "I'm not a greedy woman usually," she heard herself say as she raised herself slightly. She hooked her leg over his thigh to let him know she understood. She tested the contrast of his rougher skin and bulkier muscles with a slow movement of her thigh. "You deserve more time to get in the mood, Clint. I shouldn't have rushed you."

He looked up at her and gave her a slow, sweet kiss. "And I deserve a woman who doesn't wear boots to bed and who will stay put when a man can't run after her."

She realized she'd been prowling her boot over his bare feet. "Oh."

She sat up, pulled her boots free and settled down beside him. She gripped her robe closely and allowed her foot to find his leg—the stubble there reminded her how he had suffered in Green Tomato, how he was her warrior, her champion, her accomplice in becoming a now-woman. "I didn't mean to dominate you, Clint. To frighten you or to use you for my own primitive needs. I apologize."

She snuggled closer to him. He smelled so fine, so shower-fresh and all rugged male without cologne or after-shave. She stroked his chest, enjoying the width, the strength and the hard muscles leaping at her touch. "I know it's too soon, but I'd like to mash you flat on this air mattress, Clint. But I won't, because clearly I've intimidated you with my dominating, greedy self."

"I like a woman who takes command," Clint said in a dark, husky, encouraging voice.

She considered his statement. "That is truly strange, Clint. I thought old-fashioned males liked to call the shots, so to speak. Do you feel threatened by a woman...ah...on top?"

"I'm a now-man. I understand the need to balance a relationship. Could be there comes a time when I might be a little primitive, too." He stroked the fabric over her breast. "Would I frighten you?"

"You couldn't. I've known you forever." Excitement raced through Lilah. She could share her innermost thoughts with Clint and she wanted him to share his with her. "Clint, do you think all those positions are possible?"

He stiffened at her side and his fingers tightened gently over her breast, a possessive gesture. "Positions?"

Lilah flushed, shaken by the needs running through her. "Ah...just how primitive could you be?" she asked, testing the line of his mouth with her fingertips.

He nipped her finger slightly. "I truly don't know. I've never been revved up like what you do to me. I wouldn't want to release my needs upon you and frighten you away. You've bewitched me, Lilah. I'm under your spell."

"Bewitched?" The magical word hovered on the moonlight and she glowed. She wanted more of Clint's new verbiage and when he was silent, she knew she'd have to wring it from him. She wouldn't spare him a heartbeat of mercy.

"Tell me what you're thinking. Share yourself."

Lilah hoped she would soon taste Clint's ultimate passion. When he didn't move, she touched him lightly, just a sweeping movement over his lower stomach. Her fingers stopped and hovered above him. The miracle of their joining whizzed through her and she shivered, wanting him and uncertain how to seduce him. "You're not the only one with ideas about seduction," she whispered. "Don't worry, Clint, I'll try not to rush you before you're ready—"

In the next instant, Clint flowed over her, kissed her deeply, and while she was stunned and hunger trembled inside her, he caressed her femininity and whispered urgently, "This is how it is with me."

She cried out as he entered her slowly, fully, and pressed deeply into her. Lilah quivered beneath him, locking her fingertips to his shoulders, because she wasn't letting him get away. "My robe is still on, Clint," she told him shakily as he eased the silk flowers away to study her breasts in the moonlight.

Lilah stared at him and gripped his shoulders. She tugged his glorious chest down to her aching breasts and locked him tightly with her arms and legs. "I've never felt like this before," she whispered against his ear between nibbling it. She nipped his shoulder with her teeth, licking the small wound and tasting him.

Clint's large hands cupped beneath her bottom and lifted her higher. She locked her legs around his waist. "Talk," she demanded in an uneven whisper, digging her fingers into his taut shoulders. "I bewitch you?" she breathed, pausing to consider the depth and fullness of his entry.

He shuddered and lifted her higher and Lilah cried out, startled and realizing suddenly that she had never been taken so desperately before. Stretched to her fullest, Lilah knew then that she wanted everything Clint could give her. "I've never felt this before," she said shakily, testing herself against his strength.

But he was kissing her hungrily, his body thrusting into hers and she was tossing him back, locking him tighter into her. She gripped him with every muscle possible, held him with all her strength and clutched him because he wasn't leaving her. Lilah McCord wasn't a woman for letting a good man go, and she wanted to show Clint how much she cared about him. She returned his hunger with her own. She wouldn't allow him to rein in his needs, because she fully intended to meet him in every way. "You're giving me everything tonight, Clint Danner, right here under this moon."

"You...are...a hard woman, Lilah," he whispered roughly against her skin, thrilling her even more.

His face was hot against her throat, his breath uneven, his hands caressing as the fire grew within her and she flamed, fighting him, claiming him. She heard herself calling out something from the depths of her soul, chanting the words in magical heat, meaning them desperately. Clint shouted as if his soul had fled him, flying to the moon. She cried out, wrapped in the beauty and the fiery needs bursting within her.

When Clint's head settled to her breast, she stroked his hair and freed the joyful tears that had swelled within her. "That's how I feel about you, Lilah," Clint murmured against her skin. "Like I'll burst if I don't see you. There's the tenderness and the light-headed feeling when I'm with you, but there's this, too. As if we're burning together, a flame in one heart and one body."

"I didn't think this could happen to me, not now," she said softly, amazed at what had passed between them. How perfect he had been, how wonderful....

Her hand stopped in his hair and she clasped it, raising him to look at her. She stared at him, emotions tumbling all around her like shattered diamonds. Fear and uncertainty rose to tighten her throat. "What are you saying, Clint?"

"I love you, Lilah," he said slowly, warily, as if expecting her to push him away. "Sweetheart," he added unevenly as if testing a new lifetime word, one which he intended to use many times.

"Love," she repeated, the word echoing in her ears.

Clint pushed open the doors to Lilah's Billiards and found her immediately. He gripped her boots in his hand as he realized again how much he loved her—his sweet little Oklahoma goddess.

Pride ran through him as he watched her. Lilah was one fine piece of woman. She was smart, too, ramrodding a business into a success. She could hold her own and she had weathered the years and the hardships fallen upon her.

Lilah did look like his goddess, framed in a pool of morning light from the window as she counted a shipment of cue balls. She had a clean, ageless beauty that needed nothing to enhance it.

He pushed down the fear that had been riding him for two days—since she'd looked at him with those huge, frightened eyes and flew away to her tower. He inhaled, nodded to Old Sam's happy greeting and followed her into the storeroom. He took the large can she was lifting from a high shelf and placed it on the floor, then closed the door.

She'd hurt him, he realized. He'd given his heart to her and she'd run from him. Lilah had probably never been made love to in such a desperate, hot, hungry way—but that was how he felt, the plain simple truth of it. "I said, I love you, Lilah," he repeated, his stomach clenching with fear. "It's a lover's statement that manners say is usually answered by the love-ee."

Lilah stood very straight, facing him as he tipped back his western hat. It was good that she was a fearless woman, because Clint intended to have his say.

He dropped the boots and the sound echoed like a dynamite blast in the small shelf-lined room. "The love-ee doesn't usually fly across the meadow in her robe, running like Satan himself was after her. She should stay and call the cards. Any now-woman worth her salt knows that."

Nothing could have stopped him from continuing. "You can't just love a man... you can't just go tasting a man's soul...have him thinking love words, then say, 'La-te-da,' and pick up your red silk flowers and run away after that, Lilah McCord. You should know better."

Lilah backed against a wall. "Do you realize how we acted, Clint?" She raised her hands and spread trembling fingers before her. "I actually... I..."

She moved quickly, circling him, and jerked up his shirt to view his back. Clint held very still; he treasured each little red mark her nails had made. Lilah inhaled sharply as she moved to unbutton his collar and ease his shirt away from his throat and shoulders. Clint also treasured the light marks of her teeth on his skin. Lilah closed her eyes. "It's true. I was hoping that I hadn't acted so...engrossed in the subject. It was your fault. You said I bewitched you...and you called me a goddess. What woman could withstand that kind of talk? Especially when the man is loving her in such a deep, fierce, mind-blanking, body-heating way?"

Clint felt his tension lessen. A tiny, cheery glow lit his fears—she'd noticed the way they made love wasn't ordinary. He needed that encouragement; he'd been through two days of gut-gnawing hell. His main fear ran to Lilah loving Jeff until eternity, unable to make room in her heart for one Clint Danner. "You were pretty engrossed. So was I. But this isn't a one-night stand and you can't go running off when I'm talking intimate. It disables a man and he gets scared. I could be permanently damaged."

She shuddered and her eyes pleaded with him to understand. He didn't, but forced himself not to grab and kiss her. Lilah McCord had to make her own choices. "No, you're right," she said. "It was two nights and that makes an affair, I guess. Now I'll never get the chance to seduce you the way I had planned. We just zoomed through that part. It's gone forever, a lost moment in time. I haven't even gotten to try my new body language on you. Missy is really good at it—all those little sly looks and tilting back her head and batting her eyes at you."

"This isn't an affair," Clint said slowly, dismissing Missy from his intimate talk. "We're long-term, maybe even lifetime. We just haven't figured out the *p*'s and *q*'s of making love slower. We'll get there though. But you'll slow us down completely if you keep running off."

"I thought I was too old to feel this way. Oh, sure, I talked big and I tried to be a now-woman, but when tit-comes-to-tat, I'm scared." Lilah shook her head and leaned wearily against Clint. "I can't sleep. Clint, this is all abnormal at our ages. We shouldn't be revving up... we should be gearing down. I don't understand how I can need you so much, want you and feel so good when I'm with you. Who would think Lilah McCord would feel foofy? Just because of a lip-sucking cowboy?"

She nuzzled his chest, kissing it. "Right now, I'd like to dive into you and skip the niceties. I'm so excited and new and hungry. It isn't right. I don't seem to be able to focus on the proper step-by-step approach. I want to flirt a bit and test my body language with yours. You know—titillate your senses."

Clint stroked her back. At least he hadn't frightened her from him. "You titillate me plenty. I'm sorry I scared you."

She gripped his shirt and tugged him closer, looking up at him with a fierce frown. "It isn't you, gooney. It's me. Don't you understand that I want you every minute? That I want to... to share your life and vamp you every day and night? I want to wear you to a nubbin and love you right back up again, and I want to be with you when the loving isn't hot, but melts gently in our hearts. I want to rock on the front porch with you and watch time go by while I'm holding your hand. But in the meantime, I want to seduce the socks off you. All of this is frightening to me, Clint—I'm an organized person and I can't help grabbing you. I feel like... like... that right now, that's what I feel like."

She paused and locked her arms around his neck, tugging him down to her kiss. He allowed her to back him against the door; he died slowly when she opened his belt and jeans. Clint barely breathed as Lilah looked up at him, her eyes pleading. "I still haven't seen you in the all-together.... Except for that time in the shower and there was too much water and steam to see properly. This is all so new. I'm not a young honeymooner anymore, Clint. Things are so confusing. I thought emotions like these were for the twenty-year-olds, at least not for the over-forty crowd. *Oh, Clint, I've been married, had children and I have never, never felt so needing in my entire life.*"

"Tell me what you want," he offered gently as he eased her jeans open. "Show me."

"You," she said in a long slow, hungry sound. "Right now, right here.... See? None of this is possible and I'm still wanting everything." She frowned up at him. "It isn't just this, but right now it seems pretty important. I want to flirt with you and seduce you and... I get all soft and fluttery and damp when I just look at you. Oh, Clint, how I do ache for you," she wailed softly, shivering.

"Good enough," Clint said unevenly, his heart filling with joy.

"Clint?" Lilah asked helplessly as he lifted her bottom in his hands and joined their bodies.

Their gazes locked and Clint said slowly, "We're not the get-around-to-it-tomorrow type people, honey. We're strong people and we take what we want. We'll take it slow and hold hands and play games or anything else you want, but there will be times like this, too. Everything is just how it's supposed to be."

Lilah cried out softly and Clint kissed her with the hunger and excitement racing through him. She held on to his shoulders and leaned back, tightening her legs around his waist. She grinned slowly at him, like a conspirator of the heart. "Why, Clint. Is this vertical lovemaking? I've always—"

She paused, closing her eyes and licking her lips slowly as a trembling heat ran through their bodies. When her eyes opened, they were dark with desire. "I've wanted to try this, Clint. Thank you."

"You're welcome, and by the way, I meant what I said about loving you. I do," he returned graciously and then in a storm of heartbeats and fever, Lilah and he burst into stars and drew gently back into the darkened storeroom.

She leaned weakly against him, and he wished he could carry her off without the customers noticing. "Now, that's class A pacing," she murmured appreciatively against his chest.

Gathering her closer, Clint kissed her flushed cheek and cuddled her drooping body. "Move in with me. Share my house. You've already got my heart."

Her fingers tightened on his waist. "Live together? Us? Lilah and Clint, widow and widower, who everyone in Green Tomato knows? The town isn't over the scandal of Jessie Johnson and Elmer Friend's living together to share their late-life expenses. Our children would be shocked. People would say we're having a midlife fling. What I feel for you is solid, despite the fire and the hunger, Clint."

"We're not having any damn midlife fling." He bit out the words. "I'm not asking you to do my laundry or clean house. Our children have their lives and their loves. They'll understand and wish us well. We'll make a heck of a houseful when they all turn up at the holidays," he stated flatly so she'd know that he wanted her for herself. He'd wanted to ask her at a more romantic time. He'd wanted to ease into the idea and wrap her up before she knew what hit her. But at the same time, he wanted her to be certain she wanted the commitment to him.

And when she was gently accustomed to the idea of sharing his life, Clint had decided to ask her to marry him. He'd plant a rose garden or any other thing she wanted and bring her breakfast in the morning and ride his bike with her— And he wouldn't stop making her happy. He gently fastened her clothes and adjusted his own. He straightened her hair.

"Live together?" she repeated slowly. "Why?"

Her question nettled. "So you can seduce me, nibble on me and cry out those long, hungry purrs for no one but me," he answered. "So we can take showers together and make vertical love or any other kind of love when we want. So I can treat you in a loverlike way without the whole damn town watching my every move and people taking bets and asking me why my truck is parked by your place.... I haven't even gotten to bring you breakfast in bed—my bed—or had my I-love-you written in the sky by Lucky's Air Service. I haven't even mashed you in a bed of rose petals yet.... A man needs time and privacy to work on his intimacy skills, Lilah McCord," he finished gloomily.

"I do not make noises," she returned, studying him carefully. "Why, Clint. I've hurt your feelings, haven't I?"

"I'll live," he said, tucking her T-shirt into her jeans as it had been before they'd made love.

"So none of this is really frightening to you? At our ages? I mean this...my combustibleness?"

"I'll live," he repeated, and prayed that she felt one-tenth of his love for her. He prayed that her body already knew what her heart might someday come to feel. Because when Lilah captured him, made love to him, she was a greedy, loving woman....

"Good old Clint." She patted his chest and opened the door, stepping out lightly into the hallway. She began to hum and jog in place as if burning off excess energy.

"Right," he muttered. He braced his hand against a shelf and summoned his strength. He wondered if he'd need help getting back to his pickup. Right now, his legs weren't all that steady. Lilah would make her choices when she was ready; he'd have to wait.

That afternoon, Lilah faxed Clint her offer of a date, riding to Potsburg for the drive-in movie. She hoped he liked the present she'd sent, the leopard-print shorts and the black ones, carefully gift-wrapped in hot-pink tissue paper and secured in a box heavily wrapped in shipping tape.

She hummed as the paper slid through the fax machine. When Clint was not quite so fierce about women paying bills for their men, and off balance because she'd asked him for a date, she'd test his receptiveness to a nudist colony.

Lilah jogged in place, the physical activity helping her need of Clint. Then she decided that she was a now-woman and she could ask him in person, so she jogged out of the billiard parlor. She jogged up the street, nodded to Edward Jamison, who had swung into stride with her. She left him behind in her pursuit of Clint, her lover, her now-man.

Clint loomed over the fax machine, her message in his hands. "*I'll* pick you up at seven. That will give us time to get to Potsburg before the movie starts," he stated darkly. "*I'll* pay."

She jogged around his desk and leaped upon him, kissing him with all her might. "Wrong," she said, spearing her fingers through his hair and loving his "What hit me?" all-male look.

She kissed him again more gently, because Clint deserved time to adjust to her new mode and her loving him. His big hands tightened possessively on her bottom just the way she liked. She batted her lashes and looked up at him from under them. "Did you like my presents? Will you wear them for me?"

"Those scraps of silliness? They won't fit," he told her, shuddering slightly and holding her close.

"I have ones that match, only with lace and bras," she offered and licked her lips with the tip of her tongue. Clint's arms tightened around her as he stared hungrily at her mouth. "And I'm learning how to belly dance."

Clint staggered against the wall, still supporting her and looking like a stunned man. "I'll fit everything in them somehow," he said in a raspy tone as she stepped onto his desktop, his chair, then down to the floor. "But you're not paying my way. No righteous man would allow that. You've already got gossip flying that my business is in trouble from when you paid at the café."

Lilah looked over her shoulder to him in her new flirtatious pose. She fluttered her lashes again. "Can't you take the heat?"

When Clint muttered and moved purposely toward her, she jogged out of his office and sidestepped Edward, who was panting deeply.

"I can stand anything if I know you're happy," Clint stated darkly that night when she drove through the drive-in's ticket box and paid for them. He glanced at her chest, shimmering in her push-up bra, and groaned, sliding down into his seat. Clint proved to be a masterful drive-in lover, lifting her onto his lap and kissing her until she needed more.

He called her his goddess when she undressed for him, standing beneath the old cottonwoods near the swimming hole and Lilah moved into his arms with a sense of coming home.

When he calmed her shaking body, stroking and caressing her later, she listened to him whisper his love and held him tightly.

They lay until dawn, warmed by each other and the clothing Clint had draped over them. They dressed slowly, savoring the closeness with touches and looks that spoke of hunger and gentle ties.

"I'm not going to any damned nudist colony," Clint stated in a low outraged roar the next day. Her bouquet of roses for him shook in his hand, strangled by his fingers. Her customers stared at him.

"You still shaving your legs, boy?" Old Sam asked amiably.

Lilah moved against him, rested her head on his shoulder and stroked his chest soothingly. She waited for his arms to come around her, which they did. She stroked the taut back of Clint's neck and tugged his head down. "You're so fine," she whispered in her sexiest voice; she smiled invitingly into his scowl. "My prince."

"Prince," he muttered in an ominous tone. Then he began to grin, a disarming, brilliant wide grin that stopped her heart. "I'll bet you say that to every guy you want."

"Only to you," she whispered back, loving him.

"Now-woman or not, you're coming with me," he said unevenly. He picked her up in his arms and began carrying her down the street toward his pickup. Lilah wrapped her arms around his neck and snuggled to the chest she loved. She might as well flop her love for Clint out in front of everyone, so she wouldn't be responsible for heart attacks later. Folks in Green Tomato watched from store windows or gathered on the street. Old Sam strolled behind them, not that Lilah cared, she was too busy thinking of how she'd make love to Clint and pledge her lifetime love as she had been wanting to do.

Clint looked down at her sternly. "You can't just tell a man you love him when you're holding him tight and then forget it at other times."

"I said I love you?" she asked, momentarily confused. Though her heart was filled with love for him, she didn't remember saying it aloud.

"Right about the times when you're gripping me so tight, I know I can't wait and the last cry you give," he stated flatly. "A man likes to hear those things all the time. We're sensitive, you know."

"I love you," she said in a small, tight tone, knowing that she meant it with all her heart. "I know this isn't easy for you, either. I realize that you've had to walk through my same steps and that you'll remember your first love every time you see your sons. Just like every time I see my girls and my grandchildren, I'll know that everything is as it should be. But you are my last love, Clint. And I love you so deeply that you fill my heart."

He stopped in midstride and his fierce look softened. "There. That's more like it. When are we getting married?"

"Saturday?" she asked hesitantly. She was anxious to start her new now-woman married status. "Of course, I haven't gotten your engagement ring yet. Big Hair, Missy and Angie have been worried about you. I wouldn't want to—"

His hungry kiss stopped her thoughts. "We'll be happy, I promise," Clint said, carefully easing her around the town's flagpole and Mrs. Lang, who stood with her mouth gaping open. "You may as well know that I want my due. I want to have the proper chance to propose after dinner with candles. I'll want my down-on-one-knee moment."

"I'll want games, body language and flirtation and romance and moonlight baths and I don't want to hold back from loving you. Because I do love you, Clint Danner. You'd be frightened if you knew how much I want you right now...here on this spot. But when this fierce need subsides, I'll still be loving you."

He nodded solemnly. "See that you do."

She cuddled against him as he drove, her fierce warrior, her prince, racing her off to a realm of cherishing and loving and lovemaking.

Lilah and Clint rolled off their round honeymoon bridal-suite bed and into the mass of pillows on the floor. "Nudist colonies aren't so bad," Clint said when he could talk.

"Uh-huh. Of course, we haven't been out of our room yet," Lilah murmured against his chest. "I'm wondering just when you'll get down to the nubbin stage. When you'll realize that we're middle-aged and should be rocking on our front porch, my prince."

Clint stroked Lilah's backside in a leisurely fashion. In a richly contented deep voice, he ordered cockily, "Call me Ace, Mrs. Danner."

She batted her lashes at him and snuggled closer, stroking his lean stomach and circling his navel—a loveplay that she had discovered stopped his thoughts and shifted them nicely to the direction she wanted. "Call me your Oklahoma goddess, and I will, big boy."

Clint looked down at her tenderly, their love swirling around them. "So you've made your choice, have you?"

"You," she said firmly, stroking his cheek. She loved him more each day, with each passing heartbeat. Fate had given her two loves, each in a different way, and her future with Clint waited like an unfolding blossom. She was eager to taste her life with him. "I choose you, my prince."

* * * * *

Silhouette

SPECIAL EDITION™

SPECIAL EDITION

Stories of love and life, these powerful
novels are tales that you can identify with—
romances with "something special" added in!

Fall in love with the stories of authors such
as **Nora Roberts, Diana Palmer, Ginna Gray**
and many more of your special favorites—as
well as wonderful new voices!

Special Edition brings you
entertainment for the heart!

SILHOUETTE® Desire®

Do you want...

Dangerously handsome heroes

Evocative, everlasting love stories

Sizzling and tantalizing sensuality

Incredibly sexy miniseries like MAN OF THE MONTH

Red-hot romance

Enticing entertainment that can't be beat!

You'll find all of this, and much *more* each and
every month in **SILHOUETTE DESIRE**. Don't miss these
unforgettable love stories by some of romance's hottest
authors. Silhouette Desire—where your fantasies will
always come true....

If you've got the time...
We've got the
INTIMATE MOMENTS

Passion. Suspense. Desire. Drama. Enter a world
that's larger than life, where men and women
overcome life's greatest odds for the ultimate prize:
love. Nonstop excitement is closer than you
think...in Silhouette Intimate Moments!

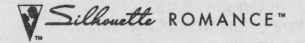

**What's a single dad to do when he needs a wife
by next Thursday?**

**Who's a confirmed bachelor to call when he finds a
baby on his doorstep?**

**How does a plain Jane in love with her gorgeous boss
get him to notice her?**

From classic love stories to romantic comedies to emotional heart
tuggers, **Silhouette Romance** offers six irresistible novels every
month by some of your favorite authors!
Such as...beloved bestsellers **Diana Palmer,
Annette Broadrick, Suzanne Carey, Elizabeth August**
and **Marie Ferrarella**, to name just a few—and some sure to
become favorites!

Fabulous Fathers...Bundles of Joy...Miniseries...
Months of blushing brides and convenient weddings...
Holiday celebrations... You'll find all this and much more in
Silhouette Romance—always emotional, always enjoyable,
always about love!

SR-GEN